# SEAL's Chance

## A CORONADO TEAM 2 NOVEL

D1362179

## Makenna Jameison

ISBN: 9798420829882

# ALSO BY MAKENNA JAMEISON

## ALPHA SEALS CORONADO

SEAL's Desire
SEAL's Embrace
SEAL's Honor
SEAL's Revenge
SEAL's Promise
SEAL's Redemption
SEAL's Command

# Table of Contents

# Chapter 1

Blowing out a frustrated sigh, Rachel Sullivan hurried across the parking lot. The handles of the plastic grocery bags bit into her hands, and she muttered under her breath. She always got a shopping cart when Keira was with her, but because her daughter was at her dad's house today, Rachel had decided to carry the bags herself. Yeah. She'd regretted that decision almost immediately.

Rachel shifted the groceries to her other hand, feeling the blood flow back to her numb fingers. She had on running shoes and her joggers. Maybe no one would notice if she literally ran through the parking lot. She struggled again as she hurried toward her SUV, then wanted to cry in frustration as the package of juice boxes broke through the flimsy plastic and fell onto the asphalt.

"Damn." She stopped, flustered, and glanced over at her car, which was still twenty feet away. She could carry the bags over and then come back for her daughter's juice. Hopefully no one would run it over in the meantime.

"I got it!" a deep voice said, and she did a double take as her neighbor Tyler came out of nowhere and reached down for the juice boxes, his muscular hand easily gripping the pack. "Here, let me grab those too," he said, lifting the remaining plastic bags full of food from her grip like they weighed nothing at all.

"Oh, thanks. I'm parked—"

"Right over there. I see it," he said with an easy grin. "I parked a few spaces down from you," he added, nodding toward his large pick-up truck. "Where's Keira?" he asked as they headed toward her SUV.

"With her dad," she muttered. Her relationship with Kyle, if you could call it that, had been fast and furious. They hadn't been able to keep their hands off one another during the few weeks they'd been together and then—poof! They'd already called things off when her period had been late and she'd realized she was pregnant.

Kyle had been an ass, insisting on a paternity test after Keira was born. He paid child support and had begun seeing her once a month since last fall. Rachel had gone to court and fought his sudden interest in visitation rights since he'd had no interest when Keira was a baby or toddler, but now he had a new girlfriend and magically wanted to be a great father.

"He's still giving you trouble?" Tyler asked, raising his eyebrows as she glanced up at him.

Tyler was tall, a little over six feet, compared to her own five-foot-eight frame. With his dusty brown hair and light blue eyes, he looked approachable. Friendly.

Some of his teammates looked intimidating with their hardened expressions and dark gazes. Tyler was literally the guy next door. He was muscular and fit, but he didn't give off the intense vibe some of his friends did.

She felt safe with him. Rachel was slender but had always been taller than her female friends. She felt almost petite next to Tyler, which was unexpected. Kyle was tall, she supposed. He never gave her that same sense of security her neighbor did though—a man she barely knew. Kyle had been edgy and intriguing when she first met him, but now he was simply a thorn in her side.

"Eh." Rachel shrugged and felt Tyler's gaze land on her. She fumbled with her keys, opening the back hatch of her SUV. "He's trying to do more with Keira now that he has a girlfriend. Never mind that he was out of her life for years and had zero interest in being a father then. Sorry," she said, her eyes landing on his concerned gaze. "I don't mean to get you involved. I could go on for hours about him and what a deadbeat dad he's been."

Tyler frowned but set the bags in the back of her SUV along with the wayward juice box package and closed her back hatch. "I don't mind if you need someone to talk to. The guy sounds like an ass."

She laughed despite herself. "Yeah. He is. We weren't together very long either. It just—happened," she said, flushing. Tyler knew how babies were made. He probably thought she was a moron for getting pregnant with a man she barely knew—who'd essentially deserted her and her child. He'd paid child support thanks to the courts, but yikes. He'd done nothing to help her when she was pregnant. Nothing to make her life easier as a new mom.

Tyler seemed competent and capable. He served in the military, didn't throw loud parties or otherwise cause trouble, and was friendly and helpful to all their neighbors. No doubt if Tyler got a woman pregnant, he'd be an active father. That was just the type of person he was. Friendly. Compassionate. He dated sometimes from what she'd seen but seemed happy living the single life. He was busy with his military career, and she respected that.

Most of the time, Rachel felt completely frazzled, running from one place to the next each day to keep her life in order. The single mom hustle was no joke. She didn't have family around to help. Her friends had pitched in occasionally, babysitting when she was absolutely desperate, but Keira was entirely her responsibility. Or she had been, until Kyle suddenly reappeared and wanted one weekend a month with her.

It was really only one day at this point. Keira hadn't spent the night at his place yet, and Rachel didn't think that Kyle wanted to deal with bath and bedtime stories. He'd spend the day with Keira, basically doing whatever the hell he wanted, then drop her off in the evening. It sucked. Especially knowing his girlfriend was around most of the time. She'd seen Carly in Kyle's expensive BMW once but still hadn't even met the woman.

"You're a great mom from what I can see," Tyler said with a smile. "You're a natural. Keira's always happy, and she's friendly and polite."

"Sorry she asks you a zillion questions," Rachel said, looking up into his light blue eyes. "She likes you, and you're good with kids."

He shrugged. "I don't know too many, but how could I not like her? She's a feisty little thing, not to mention whip smart. What's she, five or something?"

"Five going on fifteen," Rachel said, brushing her blonde hair back behind one ear. Tyler's gaze tracked her movement, and she felt herself flushing again. He wasn't interested in her. They were neighbors. Acquaintances. She hadn't dated at all since Kyle. First, she'd been unexpectedly pregnant, and then she'd been overwhelmed as a new mom. They'd finally gotten in their grove now that Keira was in kindergarten and after-school care every day. Life was finally getting easier...until it wasn't. She hated sending Keira off with Kyle for the day, but the short visits had progressively gotten longer over the past several months, and she knew at some point her daughter might spend the night or even an entire weekend there. She sensed it was coming. Rachel just had to deal with it. Bitterness and resentfulness coursed through her. Damn Kyle for being such a shitty man and father.

"Are you okay?" Tyler asked softly.

She realized she'd frozen in place, thinking about all the complications of sending her baby off alone overnight with her ex. Was Kyle even really her ex? They'd barely dated, and she'd made the mistake of falling into bed with him. She loved Keira more than anything, but goodness. Couldn't she have met a decent guy instead of that ass?

"Yeah. I'm just stressed about Keira being gone. I'm so used to being on mom duty 24/7, it's weird when her dad has her. When I'm at work, I'm busy and used to the routine, but on the weekends when she spends an entire Saturday with him, I'm just…alone. I'll get used to it."

"How long is she gone?" he asked.

"Until eight tonight. She doesn't stay overnight there yet, so I'm just running errands and trying to distract myself until he drops her off later."

A car drove down the row in the parking lot, looking for an empty space, and she realized they'd been standing there a few minutes talking. It felt nice. Usually, she had her daughter with her, so she didn't have time to stop and talk with anyone when running errands. A young child required all of her attention, and she almost didn't know what to do with her adult alone time.

"Do you want to come to a barbeque with me?" Tyler asked, those light blue eyes oddly intense as her gaze flickered back to him in surprise. "It's just with my teammates—guys from base, plus, another group of men that we work with. Some of them have girlfriends or wives, so you wouldn't be the only woman there or anything."

Briefly, she wondered how old Tyler was. She wasn't exactly young at twenty-eight but felt older than her peers with a five-year-old. Certainly, there were other young moms, but she felt out of place more often than not. Tyler looked to be around her age but led a completely different lifestyle.

"Oh," she said in surprise. "Um, maybe. I mean, where is it? Somewhere close by?" Her mind was already filling with possibilities. She didn't want to drive anywhere far away with her daughter gone for the day. What if she got hurt or sick? The whole arrangement with Keira's dad still felt new and unsettling.

Tyler didn't seem put off by her questions. His lips

quirked slightly, but she could tell he was trying to put her at ease. "It's at my buddy's house. Ace. He's having two of the teams over to his place. It's just casual. He's got a new girlfriend and wants her to meet everyone. You'll like Addison. She's really down-to-earth. No one has kids that are your daughter's age yet, but Grayson and Hailey have a baby. And hell. Harper and Logan are expecting a little one. She's due any day now."

Rachel relaxed slightly. For some reason, she'd assumed all of Tyler's friends were single Navy guys. She didn't get the player vibe from him though. Sure, she'd seen him with a woman every once in a while, but he wasn't bringing new girls home every night or anything like that. He wasn't throwing loud parties with a bunch of rowdy, single guys. He dated just like everyone else did. She'd dated...years ago. Kyle had seemed fun and exciting until she'd unexpectedly gotten pregnant. She couldn't fault Tyler for going on dates and living his life. They were just friends. Neighbors. She didn't know him too well but sensed she could trust him. Something about Tyler put her at ease.

"What time is the barbeque? I need to be back by eight—a little earlier actually. Kyle's dropping her off at my place then."

"I'll get you home in plenty of time," Tyler said with a smile. "The barbeque starts at five, and Ace only lives about twenty minutes from our apartment complex. He rents a house, so he has a large backyard to grill and host things like this. You can wear whatever—what you have on now is fine," he said, his gaze briefly sweeping over her.

Rachel felt her skin heat. She hadn't been with a

man in years, but she had to admit she liked Tyler's eyes on her, even if nothing would ever come of it. Going to a barbeque together didn't mean much. It wasn't even really a date, right? They were just hanging out with his friends. Tyler had on cargo shorts and a tee shirt, but she swore he'd look good in anything. Or nothing, she thought with a flush. Not that she was imagining him shirtless or anything. He was an attractive guy. And at the moment, she just felt flustered by his sudden attention.

"I'll wear something nicer," she said lightly. "Joggers and running shoes were just for errands. Oh. Should we bring something?" Her gaze landed back on the storefront. "I can go back and…." Her voice trailed off. Was it strange to offer to bring something to a barbeque when she didn't even know the hosts? She wasn't Tyler's girlfriend or anything.

"I was just about to grab some drinks now," he said. "I'll get some beers, and I know some of the women prefer wine or wine coolers. They'll have sodas and water, too. Is there anything you like?"

"Oh, I'm fine with whatever," she assured him.

"All right, so, I'll pick you up around four-thirty," he said, his lips quirking. "No need to tell me your address," he joked. "I'll just come over and knock."

She smiled up at him. Of course, she couldn't ever actually date the man. They were quite literally next-door neighbors. If they went out a few times and then things fizzled out, it would be awkward to live right next door to Tyler. Not that he was interested in dating a single mom like her anyway. He was just being friendly. She'd seen the women he was with. They were young, unattached. They sure didn't have the frazzled mom look that she often had going for her, not to mention the Kindergartner shadowing her every move.

"Sounds good," she said. "And thanks for your help with the groceries. I better get home and get everything in the fridge."

"My pleasure. I'll see you soon, Rachel."

He turned and headed toward the store, glancing back once over his shoulder at her. She waved and then, feeling flustered, hurried to open her car door. Tyler had just caught her watching him. The man was gorgeous—all hard lines and muscle. He wasn't overly bulky, but wow. Tyler looked like an athlete ready to spring into action. And she loved the way he made her feel like the only person in the world when they were talking. He might be laid back, but there was an intensity about him as well. He honed in on her when they were together. She was used to having her daughter around, but just now?

That blue gaze on her had made Rachel feel all sorts of unexpected things.

Shaking her head, she climbed into her vehicle. She pulled out her cell phone, making sure there were no messages from Kyle. She'd insisted he call in the event of an emergency, but otherwise she didn't usually hear from him. It was unnerving. Unsettling. The man hadn't been involved in her daughter's life for years, and now the courts let him spend an entire day with her.

Blowing out a sigh, she turned on her SUV. She'd get everything put away and then figure out what to wear to the barbeque. Tyler seemed genuine when he'd invited her along, but hopefully, he hadn't done so out of pity. They'd been friendly to one another since she and her daughter had moved in last year, but that was it. They hadn't flirted or dated. They were just neighbors.

She had too much to juggle anyway without worrying about having a new man in her life. Glancing in the rearview mirror, her stomach fluttered. She was more excited about spending the evening with Tyler than she wanted to admit.

# Chapter 2

Tyler "Trigger" Howard grinned as he walked into the grocery store. He was looking forward to the barbeque at Ace's even more after running into Rachel. Hell. He'd been interested in her for months but unwilling to do anything about it since one, they were neighbors, and two, she had a kid. Keira was cute as hell but certainly a handful. He'd come home from base more than once to see both Rachel and Keira playing outside in the evenings. Fortunately, the apartment complex had a small playground, and there was a soccer field nearby. He'd almost jogged over there to join them once when they were kicking a ball around but decided he shouldn't intrude. Rachel probably wanted some mother/daughter time after working all day. Still, he had to admit she intrigued him.

When he'd spotted Rachel coming out of the store, he hadn't been able to stop himself from walking over to say hello. And then the plastic bag had broken, and he'd swooped in to help her. Not that she needed it. She'd managed to raise a young child on her own all these years and seemed to be doing okay for herself. He wasn't sure what she did for a living, but Rachel left in business clothes every day. He liked that she was on the tall side for a woman. For some reason he'd always been attracted to women closer in height to him. He still had several inches on her, but she was the perfect height for him to easily duck down and kiss.

Damn.

He'd been tempted to step closer to her just now. With her flushed cheeks, pretty blue eyes, and that satiny blonde hair pulled back, she'd looked tempting as hell. He knew she was stressed about her daughter being gone for the day, but she'd seemed almost relaxed talking to him by her SUV. Normally her eyes were tracking Keira's movements—not that he blamed her. A rambunctious five-year-old no doubt required constant supervision. She'd looked younger than usual today, too. Rachel didn't normally wear heavy makeup, but she was fresh-faced and pretty.

His phone buzzed, and he lifted it to his ear after seeing Rob "Slinger" McPherson's name on the screen.

"Hey man, what's up?" he asked.

"I just got back from a run. I should've gone this morning but was working on my truck then. Are you headed to Ace's this afternoon?"

"Damn straight. As a matter of fact, I just invited my neighbor to come with me."

"No shit," Rob said with a chuckle. "She's the one with a kid, right?"

"Yeah. Her daughter is with her dad for the day though, and I just ran into Rachel at the store. I kind of spontaneously invited her along. I figured Addison is meeting some of the guys she doesn't know yet, and yesterday, Ace said some of Addison's friends will be there, too."

Everett "Ace" Walker was the leader of their SEAL team, one of several stationed at Naval Amphibious Base Coronado. He'd recently started dating a woman he'd met online gaming. Addison had met some of the guys, Tyler included, but would meet everyone else today. From what Ace had said, her friends were interested in meeting some single Navy guys. Not that Tyler had been interested in any women lately aside from Rachel. The guys on the other SEAL team all had wives or girlfriends, but aside from Ace, the men on their team were single.

"Which friends is she bringing?" Rob asked nonchalantly, and Tyler's lips quirked. The guys had noticed Rob had taken interest in one of Addison's friends, not that anything had come of it yet.

"I'm not sure. I think it's probably the women she works with. You met a couple of them, right?"

"Yeah," Rob said, suddenly seeming distracted. "I met Cassie and Olivia. All right. I'll catch you later then."

Shaking his head, Tyler moved through the store, grabbing some drinks and a case of beer. He went through the self-checkout line, flashing his ID at the person monitoring the area even though he was well past twenty-one, and then headed toward his pick-up truck. He'd just gotten it a year ago and was suddenly thankful he'd purchased a double cab. He assumed Keira needed some kind of booster or car seat. Not that he was planning on taking Rachel and Keira anywhere, but if he ever dated his pretty neighbor, it was a possibility. He doubted a five-year-old could ride up front.

He'd never seen Rachel with a man at all, come to think of it. Her ex was there, obviously, when he picked up Keira. Rachel didn't seem to date though or even go out with girlfriends. Her life was with her daughter.

Remembering Ace's story about how he'd wished he'd brought flowers on his first date with Addison, Tyler left the drinks in the truck and then turned and jogged back to the grocery store. It wasn't a date, per se, but he wasn't opposed to dating Rachel. If everything went as he hoped this afternoon, he'd ask her out for real. Take her to dinner one night. And making a good impression wouldn't hurt his chances. If not, well, what woman didn't like flowers?

He picked a small, colorful bouquet, checked out again, and then strode back outside to his truck. The San Diego sun was beaming down, it was a gorgeous afternoon, and he was going to spend the evening with his buddies and a beautiful woman. Nothing wrong with that.

\*\*\*

Two hours later, Tyler was knocking on the door to Rachel's apartment. He knew he was grinning like an idiot, but he was also too excited to care. How many times had he passed by her door, wishing he was doing exactly this? Tyler dated, sure, but something about this woman piqued his interest. He loved that he was getting to spend a few hours with her. Funny that if he hadn't run out to the store earlier for some drinks to bring to the party, he'd probably never have asked her to come with him.

Rachel had a turquoise doormat that said "Smile" in yellow letters and a simple wreath hanging on her front door. His own place was sparse in the way of furnishings and decorations, but he'd never felt it was lacking in anything until now. He hadn't even set foot inside Rachel's place, and it already felt homier than his own apartment. Tyler was a simple guy, happy with the basics, but he appreciated a woman's touch.

He heard soft footsteps, and then Rachel was opening the door, looking surprised as he held out the bouquet. "Hey," he said. "I brought you flowers."

"Wow, thank you." Her cheeks flushed slightly as she took the bouquet from him, and he couldn't help but run his gaze over her. She had on skinny jeans that hugged her long legs and a floral blouse. Although it clearly wasn't meant to be overtly sexy or revealing, it looked awesome on her. The swells of her breasts pushed against the fabric, and the flowy way the blouse moved somehow reminded him of lingerie. It must be the silky material, he decided. It was delicate and soft. Feminine.

Tyler wanted to wrap his hands around her hips and tug her in for a kiss, but that would be inappropriate as hell. They hadn't even gone to the party yet, and it wasn't technically even a date. She might have zero interest in him romantically, although given the hint of pink on her flushed cheeks, that didn't seem to be the case.

"Come in," Rachel said, those blues eyes meeting his. Hers were almost a deep turquoise, and combined with her soft blonde hair, she was stunning. "I need to put these in water."

"All right," he said easily, stepping into the small foyer. "Your place looks nicer than mine," he joked, taking everything in. She had paintings on the wall, an area rug underneath her coffee table, and even curtains. He'd made do with the standard apartment blinds but could see how much warmer her place felt.

She glanced back at him. "It's the same model apartment, right?"

"Yep. You just have better decorating skills. My sister visited my place once and was horrified. It's clean," he quickly added, "but the walls are bare. I think she described it as sterile," he added said with a chuckle.

"I didn't know you had a sister," Rachel said, walking toward her kitchen. Tyler stayed back, not wanting to crowd her. He heard the water running and assumed she was filling up a vase.

"Yep, she's a few years younger than me and lives on the East Coast. How about you?"

"Only child," she said, reappearing with the vase of flowers. "These are so pretty. That was so sweet of you to bring them." She set the vase down on the coffee table. Tyler noticed some toys in the corner and some crayons and coloring books on the table, but the apartment was otherwise neat.

"Keira's things are mostly in her room," Rachel said, noticing where his gaze had landed. "Honestly, she's already outgrowing a lot of toys. She's more into drawing and crafts—plus anything outdoors. Things were so crazy when she was little with baby toys everywhere and now, all of sudden, she's such a big kid. It's like you blink and they grow up," she added with a laugh.

"Well, I don't know much about kids, but I can imagine. One of the guys on the other team and his wife have a baby. I think I mentioned Grayson and Hailey earlier. That poor kid screams all the time. It's rough for all of them."

Rachel smiled. "Yeah. So did Keira. It's a lot easier now."

"I've seen you outside playing together when I get home from work. She has a lot of energy. I guess I was that way too as a kid. I could spend hours outside and never wanted to come back in."

"It's a good thing you don't have a desk job then," she joked.

"True that," he said with a chuckle. "Training can be rough some days, but I love it. I can't imagine sitting still from nine to five. I need the physical exertion."

"I bet," she said. Her eyes briefly landed on his biceps, and his chest swelled with pride. Tyler and his teammates trained hard. He wasn't huge by any means, but he did have muscles. His physique showed the efforts of their training, and he liked that Rachel noticed.

She looked away to grab her purse, but he hadn't missed the flash of interest in her eyes. She might not necessarily want to date him, given that she had a young child, but he could tell she was attracted to him. Hopefully Tyler could convince her to give him a chance. He had no way of knowing if anything would come from a few dates with Rachel, but he'd been interested every time he'd seen her so far. He'd never really thought one way or another about dating a woman with kids. It wasn't a dealbreaker by any means, but if she didn't want to complicate her life any further by dating, he would understand that, too.

It would kill him if she did start to date other guys and he'd have to watch the lucky bastard given that they were neighbors. She deserved to be happy, so he'd deal, but damn. When he'd thought her ex was her boyfriend, Tyler realized just how much he was interested in her. She'd been off limits in his mind, and when he realized she was available?

It was like he'd won the damn lottery.

Rachel was the total package—smart, funny, caring, and gorgeous to boot. He loved her long, blonde hair and the way she was always friendly and smiling. Some women were drama queens, but he could tell she was too busy for that. She had work and her little girl to worry about. Tyler was amazed some other man hadn't swooped in and snatched her up.

"Are you ready to head out?" he asked as she slung her purse over her shoulder and pulled out her sunglasses and keys. "I already stashed the beers and drinks in my truck, so we're good to go."

"Yeah, I'm all set. It's easier without a kiddo in tow. I almost feel like I'm forgetting something," she said, looking around.

"I figured. Despite the rogue juice boxes in the parking lot, you looked more relaxed than usual—not that I blame you," he quickly added. "Kids are a handful."

"That's putting it mildly," she joked.

Tyler pulled open her door and stepped into the breezeway, watching as she locked the door behind them. His stomach twisted slightly as she pulled her key from the lock. Even though they lived in a safe area, she only had the standard lock on her door. He'd gotten permission from the landlord to install a sturdier deadbolt on his. He deployed frequently, so he felt better knowing his belongings were secure when he was gone. Why make his place an easy target?

He didn't like that Rachel didn't have a deadbolt though. Aside from her own safety, she had her daughter to worry about. She shouldn't have to worry about some asshole breaking into her place because the apartment complex hadn't put in the highest quality lock on the market. "I installed a stronger lock on my door," he said casually as they walked down the hall. "The standard issue ones the apartment complex used aren't as sturdy."

"Oh yeah? This one seemed sufficient, but maybe I should check and see if I can do that as well. I'd feel better knowing no one could get inside."

"I should've mentioned it before," he apologized.

Rachel lifted a shoulder. "We're neighbors. It's not like you were obligated to tell me how to secure my apartment. I'm an adult, too," she teased gently.

"Well, I should have," he said, glancing over at her. "Anyway, I'm glad you can come with me to the barbeque. My teammates are cool, but I think you'll like the women there, too."

"So, all of you guys are Navy SEALs?" she asked in a low voice as they walked toward his pick-up truck. Tyler knew he'd mentioned it to her at some point. He didn't want her to be worried if his buddies ever dropped by, and she kept an eye on his place during his frequent deployments. Sometimes she'd grab a package if it showed up at his door or pull the random flyer off so it wasn't obvious no one was home. There'd been several occasions where he'd even given her some of his extra food rather than tossing it all out. Not that she couldn't afford to buy what she needed, but it seemed silly to dump out all his milk when Rachel and Keira were right next door and would use it.

They'd been…neighborly. He wanted to kick himself for assuming she was with Keira's dad though. He'd assumed they were having trouble given their bickering but had always thought they were a couple. He'd had no clue until recently that she hadn't even seen the guy in years.

"Yeah, we're all SEALs. My team will be there, as well as another one from base. The guys on the other team all have wives or girlfriends. My teammates are mostly single."

"Mostly. You're not secretly married, are you?" she joked.

He chuckled. "Negative. I'd think you'd have noticed that living right next door."

"Touché. I'm just kidding. I'm kind of nervous about being around a group of Navy SEALs though. I don't know much about the military, aside from the fact that you're gone a lot. I don't want to say the wrong thing."

"I'm with them when we go on missions. There's no need to be nervous," he assured her. "We can be intense sometimes when we're training, but we like to relax and have fun just like everyone else. You've probably even seen some of the guys coming by my place a time or two. We're competitive as hell, but it's all in good fun."

"Yeah, I guess you're right," she said.

"Of course I am," he replied, smiling down at her. She looked up at him in surprise and then burst into laughter. "Don't worry, they're all cool. Ace and his girlfriend Addison are pretty new as well. She recently moved into his place."

"Oh really?"

"Yeah, and she doesn't know the guys that well either."

Tyler helped her into his pick-up truck, catching a whiff of the faint, clean scent of her perfume. She smelled like fresh air and sunshine, and damn if it wasn't hard to resist ducking down and breathing her in. That would've been inappropriate as hell though, so instead his gaze lingered on her a moment longer than it should've as she buckled her seatbelt, and then he was shutting the passenger door and rounding the front of his truck.

"I feel bad that I'm not bringing anything to the party," she said as he started the engine. Tyler's gaze flicked toward her. The floral blouse clinging to her breasts was sexy as hell, but he didn't stare. Still, he couldn't help but imagine her in some sexy floral lingerie someday.

She brushed her blonde hair behind her ears, looking slightly nervous for a beat. She had three tiny earrings in each ear, he realized. It was sexy and unexpected. What other surprises did she have?

"I already grabbed beers and some wine coolers. We're good," he assured her. She still looked slightly uncertain. "You can carry one of them if it makes you feel better," he said with a wink. "Although I'd rather do the heavy lifting myself."

"How much did you buy?" she asked with a laugh.

"Just a case of beer and pack of wine coolers. Ace is always hosting stuff, so I figured it's the least I can do. He's got a house and big backyard, whereas— well, you know how big our apartments are."

"That I do. They're even smaller with a five-year-old. Trust me on that one," she said, smiling.

Tyler pulled his truck out of the parking lot and onto the road, suddenly feeling slightly nervous. He lived alone and was used to having his own space, his own schedule. He trained and went where the Navy sent him on ops, but his life was his own. What did Rachel think of a single guy like him? He wasn't exactly the immature teenager he'd been when he first joined the Navy, but hell. He wasn't a parent either. He respected her and hoped the feeling was mutual. It's not like he was throwing wild parties at his bachelor pad or something.

It felt both comfortable and exciting having Rachel here in his truck. He'd known her for nearly a year, and it almost felt like he'd finally asked out the girl he had a crush on at school. He knew some things about her, and always looked forward to seeing her smile, but it was still exciting and new doing something together.

"How long have you been in the Navy?" she asked.

"Since I turned eighteen, so eleven years. I can't believe I'll be thirty next year," he added with a chuckle.

"Yeah, that is old," she joked. He glanced over and caught the twinkle in her blue eyes. "I'm only twenty-eight."

"Ha ha. Ace turns thirty before me, so I plan to give him a hard time. I need some good jokes or whatever. He's our team leader, so he's not going down easy."

"Yeah, I'm sure he'll love that," she said, jokingly rolling her eyes as he chuckled. "And he still wants us to come over today?"

"Of course. We all like ribbing one another. It's kind of like having a group of brothers around all the time."

"You guys sound close."

"Yep. We have to be. We train together, deploy together, and of course hang out together on the weekends. Usually, I'm alone at these things though, so I'm glad you're coming with me today."

Her mouth parted slightly in surprise. Did she think he always brought a date with him? He'd dated some over the past year since Rachel had moved in, and Tyler knew she'd seem him with a woman a time or two. Nothing had ever come from it though, and he was long past the days of taking a woman home just for the night.

They talked more on the drive over to Ace's house, and he learned that Rachel was a receptionist for a law firm. She worked long hours keeping up with the schedules of the attorneys, and he could tell that she felt guilty for not always spending as much time as she wanted with her daughter.

Tyler loved how open she was. She cared about Keira, of course, but was hardworking and had supported herself and her daughter for years. It was refreshing. Some women he'd dated in the past were overly into themselves or the fact that he was a Navy SEAL. They wanted to show him off to their friends but were shallow and superficial. He'd gotten more selective in who he dated over the years, and for good reason.

He could tell Rachel was down-to-Earth. Real. He planned to pay for their dates when they went out, but he got the sense she wasn't the type of woman who'd automatically expect him to. That made him want to spoil her all that much more. She'd been genuinely surprised that he'd brought her flowers, and he loved that just a simple gesture like that had made her smile.

"All right, this is our exit," he said, flipping on his turn signal and heading for the ramp. "We'll be there in about five minutes. Don't be nervous," he said, glancing over at her.

"How could you tell I was nervous?" she asked in disbelief.

He lifted a shoulder. "I pay attention. You're hard to ignore, Rach," he said softly. He glanced over at her for a beat and caught the surprise in her blue eyes. "And you bite your lower lip when you're worried about something," he added, glancing in his side mirror before merging into traffic.

"Oh my God, I do, don't I?" she asked, suddenly raising her hands to her face in surprise. He could see she was flushing, embarrassed that he'd noticed. Tyler had paid attention to her over the past year, apparently more than she realized. He was trained to be observant in general, but how could he not notice everything about his gorgeous neighbor?

He chuckled. "It's cute as hell."

"Oh stop. It is not."

He laughed harder. "Yes, it is. You're gorgeous, and it reminds me that you're human and get nervous just like the rest of us."

"Tyler. Of course, I'm human," she mock-chastised. "I'm a rather embarrassed human at this point though."

"Sorry. It's just that I was a little nervous myself to ask you out today. I realize this was totally spontaneous, since we ran into each other in the parking lot earlier, but I'm thankful for those flimsy grocery bags. It gave me an excuse to talk with you longer, and now? You're sitting beside me in my truck."

She huffed out a small laugh, still looking slightly embarrassed, but he could see she was smiling again as he glanced over. "Yeah, me too. And I'm sure Keira will be happy that you rescued her juice boxes."

"Anytime, sweetheart," he said with a wink.

# Chapter 3

Rachel nearly did a double-take at the large house Tyler pulled up to. She'd assumed his friend was around their age, but most people she knew were still in apartments or small homes. This place was big enough for a family with lots of kids. Tyler caught the expression on her face as he parked along the curb. "Ace rents this place. I think he got tired of having roommates and wanted a house. He enjoys having space to have everyone over, so it works."

"I didn't mean to gawk," she said with a small laugh. "I'm used to my tiny two-bedroom apartment."

"Yep. Same. I can't imagine wanting a house or yard until I get married and have kids but—"

"You want kids?" she asked.

Tyler chuckled. "Why do you look so surprised? Sure, someday. Eventually, I'll get married and have a family. I just need to meet the right girl first." He winked, and she felt her skin heat. Certainly, he didn't mean he wanted to marry her. They were friends. Neighbors.

It was hard to even imagine dating a man like Tyler. He had a busy military career and seemed like the type of man who enjoyed taking charge. She was used to doing everything on her own. She made decisions for her and her daughter, handled all of her own finances, got dinner on the table every night after a long day of work, ran errands, and took care of tasks like taking her car to the shop to get the oil changed. She juggled a million different things.

Tyler worked hard as well—no doubt he had to as a Navy SEAL. He wasn't overbearing, but she could tell he was a man who liked to take charge and control his surroundings. He'd mentioned the lock on her apartment door, hadn't he? And he'd grabbed drinks to bring tonight without needing any input from her. Not that grocery shopping required her help—but still. She was used to dealing with a young child, to planning every last detail of their lives. She had to be organized getting them off to work and school each day.

She almost didn't know what to do with Tyler handling details for this evening. Sure, bringing drinks to a party was minor in the grand scheme of things, but when she was used to doing everything herself? It was easy to appreciate the little things he did. The flowers. Noticing she could use a sturdier lock. Goodness, he'd probably help her install one if she asked, not that she'd burden him with that.

It would be nice to spend a few hours with him today. Then later…Kyle would bring Keira back home, and life would return to normal.

"You're thinking too hard over there," Tyler joked,

opening his door. "Stay put. I'll come around and help you out." She debated just climbing out herself, but it was a sweet gesture. She couldn't fault him for being a nice guy. And the fact that he made her heart pound?

She swallowed, watching him round the front of his truck. Tyler's short sleeves showed off his biceps and muscled forearms. Tyler was hot as hell.

A moment later, Tyler was opening her door. He reached for her hand, helping her to step down from his truck, and she swore sparks shot through her at his touch. His large, warm hand clasped around her own made her feel all sorts of things she shouldn't. First, she didn't have time to date. Even if Keira kept going to her dad's, right now it was only one Saturday a month. Second...she supposed she did have another reason. It was hard to think of it now though when Tyler's muscular hand was holding her own and she had six feet of solid man in front of her.

Tyler smelled faintly of aftershave, but it was his fresh, earthy scent that made her blood heat. He was over two-hundred pounds of solid male and exactly the perfect amount of muscular—athletic but not intimidating. Briefly, she wondered what it would feel like having those strong arms wrapped around her. Her hand clasped in his felt oddly right. He was just helping her out of his large truck though. When she was all the way out, he dropped her hand and was closing the door. She instantly missed the feel of his warm hand wrapped around her own. God. She hadn't even so much as kissed a man in years. She needed to chill out. He was just being polite.

Tyler grabbed the drinks he'd brought and then rested his free hand on the small of her back as he guided her to the front door. A shiver raced down her spine at his touch. For a woman who hadn't been on a date in years, Tyler's attentiveness was bringing back all sorts of unexpected feelings.

She'd already known he was a nice guy, not to mention incredibly good-looking, but yikes. She was in trouble if he set his sights on her. She didn't think she'd be able to resist his charm. Tyler was easygoing, friendly, not to mention cute as hell. She doubted he'd like being called cute, but he was. And she loved how he seemed to get along with everyone.

Another couple was right inside when they walked in, and Tyler briefly introduced her. He stashed the drinks in the fridge, and she spotted the backyard full of people through the large windows. A big guy was manning the grill, and a pretty, petite brunette was at his side. There was a table full of food, another overflowing with drinks, and she'd seen from the contents of the kitchen that there was extra of everything. It was a big group, but everyone was talking and laughing. She felt comfortable here.

"That's Ace and Addison," Tyler said with a nod, catching her looking at the couple by the grill. "It looks like just about everyone else is here already."

"Are we late?" she asked, suddenly worried.

"No, we're right on time," he assured her. "Let me introduce you to some of my friends and get you a drink." They walked across the family room, with Tyler pushing open the French doors leading to the patio. "Hey guys, we're here!" Tyler called out.

"Trigger!" Ace said. "I was wondering where you were. And who did you bring?"

"This is my neighbor, Rachel. It's a long story, but I hope you don't mind that she's here."

"Of course not," Ace said as he and Addison walked over. The man was huge, even taller and more muscular than Tyler. He was somewhat intimidating, but when he smiled, the dimple in his cheek softened him a bit. "I'm Ace," he said, holding out a large hand. "And this is my girlfriend, Addison."

The brunette said hello, shaking Rachel's hand, and they all chatted a few minutes. "Grab some food and drinks," Ace said. "We've got plenty of everything. I need to go flip the burgers."

"We will," Tyler said. "I just want to introduce Rachel to some of the guys first."

"Why'd he call you Trigger?" she asked as they walked away.

Tyler's lips quirked. "We all have nicknames. Ace's actual name is Everett. I don't think I've ever heard anyone call him that—maybe his parents," he added with a chuckle. "Most of the guys go by their real names, but either works."

She gave him the side-eye. "Do I even want to know why your nickname is Trigger?"

"I'm a good shot," he said modestly. "I got the nickname after I went through BUD/S, and it stuck. I won't go into details, but we're obviously in dangerous situations when we go on missions. Speed and accuracy are crucial."

"I don't know anything about guns or weapons. I can't even imagine what types of situations you deal with. Well, I can—I just don't want to. Sitting in an office dealing with a bunch of lawyers is dangerous enough for me," she joked.

"There's no need for everyone to put themselves in danger. That's what we're there for—to go in where others can't."

She frowned, not liking the sound of that. Of course, she appreciated members of the military. They literally put their lives at stake when deployed. It was the same with first responders here in the U.S. They were willing to put their own lives on the line to help others. She couldn't imagine ever having a risky career like that—even less so now that she was a mom. Keira was her entire world. Sacrificing yourself for your child wasn't the same as being willing to take that risk for complete and total strangers though. Yet Tyler and his friends did exactly that every time they left for missions.

"You don't need to worry about me," Tyler said in a low voice, seeming to sense her distress.

She raised her eyebrows, and he chuckled. "I recognized that look. When you're outside and Keira is doing something dangerous, you get that same expression on your face."

She looked at him in bewilderment. "How did you ever notice that?"

"I noticed you," he said, his light blue eyes heating as he looked down at her. She searched his gaze, sensing his sincerity. He had noticed her. Maybe he'd stood back and never acted on it, maybe they'd just been friends, but he'd noticed more than she'd realized. It was flattering to know she had the attention of a man like Tyler. She'd been so busy with her daughter, she hadn't really given him much thought. He was the cute guy next door, busy with his own life.

And here he'd been playing close attention all along.

"Trigger! Who's your lady friend?" a tall guy asked as he sauntered over. Rachel blinked, looking away from Tyler to take in the new guy coming their way. He was around Tyler's height, with dark hair, brown eyes, and a short beard. There was a spark of mischief in his expression, and she swore Tyler stiffened slightly.

"She's off-limits, Havoc."

The guy—Havoc—winked at her. "Now, now, we'll let her decide that, won't we? I'm Owen," he said, holding out a hand. "Or Havoc, as everyone calls me. Whatever you've heard is no doubt all true. I didn't know Trigger had a girlfriend."

"We're neighbors. I'm Rachel," she said, shaking his hand.

A flash of recognition crossed his face, but then he grinned and began talking about Tyler. Had Tyler told his teammates about her? That seemed…far-fetched at best. What on Earth would he have said? As soon as she'd mentioned they were neighbors, though, Havoc had seemed to know who she was. He joked around with her another minute and then walked over to several women who seemed to be there without a date.

"I think those are Addison's friends," Tyler explained, nodding toward them. "I haven't met them yet."

"Havoc sure seems to know the darker-haired one." The woman was already glaring at him, talking a mile a minute. He seemed to enjoy the attention though.

"Huh. That he does. I guess I shouldn't be surprised. He'll chat up anyone."

"Hey Trigger," another guy said as he walked up, a bottle of beer clutched in one hand. With his dark hair, green eyes, and chiseled features, he somehow seemed more intense than the others. Tyler was strong but relatively easygoing. This guy just seemed lethal. "You must be Rachel. I'm Rob McPherson, one of his teammates."

Rachel shook hands with him and then cocked her head to the side. "Let me guess. Rob "Rifle" McPherson? Or maybe "Romeo"? It has the alliteration thing going for it at least. I know— Renegade?"

Rob chuckled, exchanging an amused glance with Tyler. "Negative. The guys call me Slinger."

Her gaze darted toward Tyler, who chuckled at her confused expression. "As in a gun-slinger. Rob's an excellent shot as well. But don't worry, we only aim at the bad guys."

"Phew," she joked, pantomiming wiping sweat off her brow. Although she didn't doubt what he said was true—they only fought the bad guys—the guy still seemed a little intimidating. He was intense in a way Tyler wasn't. "It's hard to keep everyone straight with the regular names and nicknames."

"You can just call me Rob," he said, those green eyes landing on her again. "And it's good to finally meet you. Trigger won't admit it, but we all know he had a beautiful neighbor. He might've mentioned you once or twice." Her cheeks flushed, and he winked, much to her surprise. She watched his gaze land on the blonde woman near Havoc, and he stiffened slightly. "Excuse me. I'm going to say hi to Cassie and make sure she's okay."

"I guess the blonde is Cassie," Rachel said, watching him head over to the ladies near Havoc. She looked back at Tyler. "You told your teammates about me?"

"Let's grab a drink. And yes, I told the guys about you."

"What did you tell them?" she pressed. "That you have a single mother living next door? That my five-year-old pesters you with all sorts of questions, but you're always a good sport about it?"

"Negative. I might've complained that you had a boyfriend—until I realized he was your ex," Tyler clarified, flashing her a grin. "I'll admit that I'm attracted to you, Rach. I was thrilled when you moved in last summer. The person who lived there before was a sixty-year-old divorcee. She was polite, but it was like having my mom living next door."

"Hmmm. And a single mom was more your style?"

His eyes twinkled in amusement. "A beautiful woman who happened to also be a single mom? Yeah, you could say that. I'd love to take you out on an actual date sometime—without these guys around," he said, gesturing to the group in the backyard. "I realize that we're next-door neighbors though. If you'd rather stay friends, I can respect that. I'd never want to make you uncomfortable."

"You want to date me."

It was Tyler's turn to laugh. "Why do you look so surprised?"

They walked up to the table filled with drinks, and she poured herself a glass of white wine as Tyler popped the cap off his beer. "Did you not hear what I just said? Frazzled single mother? Apparently, you've been paying attention to me all along, and I was too clueless to realize it." She took a sip of her wine and eyed him.

"I thought you were with Kyle," Tyler admitted.

"I'm sorry he's causing trouble for you, but I'm definitely not sorry that I finally realized you weren't together. I'd be crazy not to ask you out and see if this goes anywhere. Even if we just chat a few minutes, it always brightens my whole day, Rach. Work can be stressful as hell, but seeing you makes me smile."

"Tyler...geez," she said, flushing. "I love seeing you too, but, wow. I kind of always thought you weren't interested."

"I'm interested. I understand that living next door to each other could complicate things a bit though, so if you'd rather not go there, I'll back off. We can just be friends."

"Tyler, I haven't been on an actual date in years."

"So? It's like riding a bicycle. You don't forget."

"Did you really just compare dating you to riding a bicycle?" she asked with a laugh.

Tyler moved closer, smiling down at her. He reached out and brushed a stray piece of hair back from her face, and she swore she felt the touch of his fingertips burning into her skin. They were at the barbeque together. This was a date, whether she wanted to call it one or not. And it felt...good. She liked spending time with him. She loved the heat that coursed over her skin every time he was near. Knowing that Tyler had told his friends about her made her suspect he'd been watching her more closely than she ever imagined. He'd never done anything to make her uncomfortable though. Some men would've blatantly shown their interest, ogling her. Tyler had been paying attention, but he was always polite and respectful.

"Maybe I did," he said, drawing her mind back to

the present. "Let's grab some food." She glanced toward the platter of burgers and hotdogs that Ace was setting on the table. "You don't have to decide anything about us dating right now, Rach. But now that my teammates have busted me, I can admit I'm interested in you in more than a neighborly sort of way. I'm not sure if I should kick Rob's ass for that or thank him. Maybe both."

She shook her head, trying to hide her smile. It was flattering that Tyler wanted to date her, but despite the fact that she'd lived next door to him for almost a year, she really didn't know him that well. What if he expected her to jump into bed after a date or two and then she had to see him every morning after that? She needed to take things slowly.

Did he think that because she'd had a child fairly young, she'd be an easy lay? Although she didn't get that impression, she didn't know for sure. He could act totally different when they were alone. It would suck to think she'd met a nice guy only to find out he was only after getting into her pants. She was jumping way ahead of herself though.

"Those are some of the guys on the other SEAL team," Tyler said, nodding across the yard. "Ace is our team leader, and Raptor heads up another group. The blonde woman next to him is his wife. I'll introduce you to everyone this afternoon, but don't worry if you can't keep all the names straight."

"There are a lot of you," she said in amazement, looking around.

Tyler chuckled. "Yep. There are even more of us now that the other team all has girlfriends or wives. Things have calmed down a bit over the years."

"I can imagine," she said with a smile. "I've seen

some of the younger military guys on the beach, and they seem a bit wild. There aren't any kids here though."

"Ghost and Hailey have a baby," he said, pointing to a couple she hadn't noticed. Rachel realized there was a sleeping baby in the woman's arms. "Keira would fit right in."

"She'd have all your friends running around playing soccer with her."

He laughed. "They could use someone to whip them into shape. I'd like to see Havoc taking orders from a five-year-old. It would be amusing if nothing else."

"Oh goodness. Even if I don't remember anyone else here, I remember him. He seems like a handful."

"Understatement of the year," Tyler said with a smirk. Her phone buzzed as they headed toward the table of food, and she pulled it from her purse, frowning.

"Is everything okay?" Tyler asked, catching the expression on her face as she read the text. He paused to wait by her, and she appreciated that he didn't simply rush off to grab a burger. Not that she'd expected him to, but she'd learned the hard way that some men were selfish, always putting their own needs first.

"It's Kyle," she muttered. "He wants to know why Keira won't eat anything for dinner. They took her to a freaking sushi restaurant. Good grief. I'm sure some 5-year-olds might eat that—"

"But not most of them. Why would he think a Kindergartener would eat that?" Tyler asked, looking annoyed on her behalf. "I don't even have kids and realize most would be happy with some chicken

43

nuggets."

"Because he's clueless and hasn't been involved in any part of her life," Rachel said. "And now he's calling me." She shook her head, flustered, and swiped the screen to answer the call. She mouthed 'thank you' to Tyler as he wordlessly took the wine glass from her hand. "Hi. What's wrong?"

"Keira's crying and wants to come home early. I can drop her off in twenty minutes," Kyle said.

"She's crying?"

"She was. She'll be okay, but she wants to come home."

"I'm not even at home right now. Did she eat anything?"

"No. We ordered a whole platter of sushi, and she refused to touch it."

Exasperation rose within her. "Kyle, she's five. Of course, she's not going to eat that. Why couldn't you have taken her to McDonald's or something? Let me talk to her."

"Carly took her to the restroom. I figured that's better than bringing her into the men's room with me."

Rachel clenched her jaw, growing more frustrated. Although that was probably true, she didn't want her upset child to have to go into the bathroom with a woman who was essentially a stranger. Would she know to stay with her? Would she wait outside, assuming a five-year-old could take care of things herself?

Keira had only recently started spending an entire day with her father, so it's not like she could know Carly very well either. Although Rachel would've preferred for his girlfriend not to be in her daughter's life at all, she didn't get a say in the matter. The court had decided that Keira's dad deserved visitation rights, and that was that. If his new girlfriend was around, there wasn't much she could do about it.

"Fine. I'll head back home and meet you there in twenty minutes. I assume you're not staying to eat sushi?"

Her gaze flicked to Tyler, and she saw that he was processing her end of the conversation. It was too bad she'd have to leave the party to go home, but that was life. He could hang out with his friends while she called a cab or something.

"No. We didn't eat," Kyle said. "I ended up just paying the bill and wasting all that food. I'll take Carly out somewhere for dinner after we drop off Keira."

"Wonderful."

"Yeah, there's an awesome Italian place we've been wanting to try. We can have a nice, quiet dinner and order a bottle of wine or two."

"Sounds lovely," she said, wanting to reach through the phone and throttle him.

"Absolutely. Work was crazy this week, and I'm worn out after having Keira all day. She's got a lot of energy. I could use a few hours to relax and unwind. I know Carly loves when I spoil her. We've been wanting to try this restaurant for a while. See you soon."

She blew out a frustrated sigh as she ended the call, unwelcome tears smarting her eyes. Her ex was still as much of an ass as he'd always been. He hadn't had time for a child before, and he barely made time for Keira now. Whatever his girlfriend wanted, he went along with, but it was clearly all for show. He hardly seemed concerned that his own child was upset. "He's such a conceited jerk," she muttered, shoving her phone back into her purse.

"You need to get home?" Tyler asked, handing her back her glass of wine.

She looked at him apologetically. "Yeah, but we just got here. I can call a cab. Kyle's going to drop her back off at my apartment."

"I'll drive you home. Maybe we can order a pizza and all eat together."

"But your friends and the party," she said, looking up at Tyler and then around the crowded backyard. "I'd feel bad if you have to leave so soon because of me. We didn't even eat anything yet. You'd get to stay longer if I hadn't come with you today."

Tyler took a pull of his beer. "I don't mind. I wanted to spend time with you, so we'll hang out together back home instead. I'll order pizza, and it should get there right around the time we make it back."

"You're serious."

"Of course, I'm serious, Rach. I'm not going to make you take a cab back home. I drove you here, didn't I? I'm not the type of guy who would just leave you somewhere. We'll hang out with my buddies some other time. It's a gorgeous night. Maybe we can kick a soccer ball around the field after we eat. I don't have one, but I've seen you guys out there before."

"Well, Keira would love that. I feel like I'm ruining your night though."

"Not at all," he assured her. "Let me just tell Ace we're leaving. We can order pizza on the way back."

"Yeah, okay," she said, watching as Tyler strode over to his friend. Without missing a beat, he'd been totally okay with their plans for the night completely changing. She loved how easygoing he seemed to be, but then again, this was only one evening. Life with a child was always unpredictable. She'd go with it for now though. Maybe Kyle had done her a favor. If Tyler couldn't handle a night of pizza with her and her daughter, then there'd be no point in actually dating the man. She and Keira were a package deal. She wasn't the type of parent who'd constantly be sending her child off with a babysitter or nanny while she went about her life. She wanted to spend time with her, and if she eventually dated, the guy would have to be okay with that, too.

Tyler glanced over at her while talking to his friend, those blue eyes meeting hers, and she swore her heart stuttered. The evening sun lit the backyard in warm light, and Tyler looked like her own personal gift sent from above. He was handsome and athletic but genuinely nice, too. She knew some men hated being called nice, but in his case, it was true. He was a friendly, easygoing type of guy—the kind everyone liked.

And as for the fact that he made her heart pound?

Well, she'd just have to wait and see what happened.

# Chapter 4

"The pizza will be here in ten minutes," Tyler said, glancing over at Rachel as he sat in the living room of her apartment, his legs crossed. "I gave them your address instead of mine. I hope that's alright. I figured that'd be easier since we're waiting here."

"Yeah, that's fine," she said distractedly, glancing again at her phone. Rachel worried her lower lip, her teeth sinking into the plump bottom. He hated that she already looked more stressed than she had just an hour ago. No doubt having Kyle throw a wrench in their plans for the evening had frustrated her to some extent, but he could see she was worried about her daughter. The guy sounded like an idiot. Who took a five-year-old kid out for sushi anyway?

"He just texted me. They're running late because they stopped to get Carly an iced coffee. Heaven forbid she wait a few minutes until they dropped off my daughter. Ugh." She shook her head, running a hand through her blonde hair. "I'm sorry I'm stressing out. I'm just frustrated."

"It's fine," he assured her. "I'd be upset too if my kid was in a similar situation—if I had a kid, that is. Have you met this woman? She's your ex's girlfriend?"

"No. I haven't met her yet. That's part of the reason this bothers me. I knew Kyle had a girlfriend, but at first, he'd just come and pick up Keira himself. At the very beginning, the visitations were supervised, because Keira didn't even know him."

"What an ass," Tyler muttered. He saw Rachel's gaze flick to him in surprise. "Sorry, it's just hard to imagine what type of man would abandon his child."

"You don't need to apologize," Rachel assured him. "I'll never regret having Keira, but of course Kyle is another story. And yeah, he is a total ass. He told me earlier that after he drops off Keira, they're going to some fancy Italian place to relax because he's tired. Tired after one day with her. He didn't even feed her dinner." She looked toward the door. "Anyway. I doubt Carly would've even been with them tonight when Kyle dropped her back off, except the dinner got cut short."

A knock on the door had her jumping. "That's the pizza," Tyler said as he rose. "I'll get it."

"Oh, let me grab my purse and give you some cash."

"No need," he said easily as he crossed the room. "I already paid." He pulled open the door, taking the two boxes from the delivery driver, when he heard Keira's shout from down the hallway.

"Hi Mr. Tyler!"

He grinned, trying to ignore the man at her side. If he'd understood correctly, Kyle had been a musician when he'd briefly dated Rachel. He'd been too busy with his gigs to worry about Rachel or his unborn child, so he'd basically abandoned them. And since the girl barely knew her own father, she was racing toward Tyler right now. "Are we all having pizza together? Yay! I'm so, so hungry. I'm starving! Are you eating with us?"

"That I am, kiddo. Let me carry these inside."

He strode back into Rachel's apartment, letting Kyle watch in surprise as Keira went with him without so much as a goodbye to her father, talking a mile a minute. Tyler was bigger than the other man. Kyle had the edgy, rocker thing going for him, but he looked skinny. Hopefully he wasn't into illegal drugs or something like that. If this guy was spending time with Keira, maybe Tyler should look into his background. They could run a background check, of course, but Ace could dig around and see what he could find. A computer expert, he could get in and out of systems without anyone being the wiser.

"Carly's down in the car," he heard Kyle saying to Rachel. "She had a headache after missing dinner." Tyler clenched his jaw, willing himself not to say anything as he set the pizza boxes down in the kitchen. The guy seemed more worried about his girlfriend than his own kid. Keira hadn't eaten dinner yet either. The irony was, Kyle didn't even seem to realize what a dick he was. Not that Tyler was any sort of expert on children, but hell. It wound him up that Kyle seemed more concerned about a grown woman eating dinner late than an innocent kid.

Rachel talked with her ex a moment longer then closed the door, coming into the kitchen. "Hi sweetheart!" she said. Her daughter raced toward her, giving her a big hug, but then was back to talking to Tyler again about the pizza. Rachel was looking between Tyler and Keira with a smile on her face, and he loved that she already seemed happier. It was obvious she didn't like Kyle, but Tyler would do what he could to show her he was a good man. The evening might not have gone how he'd expected, but he was okay with it. They'd eat, and then maybe he and Rachel could hang out for a bit later on after Keira's bedtime, assuming she wanted him to stay.

She reached up into the cupboard, grabbing two glasses for them and a plastic cup for her daughter. He tried to ignore the way her jeans stretched over her heart-shaped ass, quickly looking away.

Rachel was gorgeous.

He shouldn't be standing here ogling her though. They needed to eat. And then he had an energetic five-year-old to kick a soccer ball around with after they all chowed down on pizza. Anything else would have to wait.

\*\*\*

"She's down for the night," Rachel said later on, padding into the living room of her apartment. She'd kicked off her shoes at some point, and Tyler could see the hot pink polish on her toenails. It was somehow both sweet and sexy. Rachel was fairly low-maintenance. She didn't wear a lot of makeup or fuss over her hair. He loved the tiny earrings and nail polish she had on though. The little touches of her personality made him want to know more. She was feminine and pretty. He loved hanging out with her, too, but he had to admit he was also attracted as hell to her. He'd love to take her out sometime, but obviously that wasn't happening tonight. Pizza and a cold beer had been fun, too, just not what he'd expected when they'd originally headed to the barbeque.

Havoc had texted him earlier, making some smartass remark about leaving early to get lucky. Right. That had been so far from the truth it was almost comical.

Although they hadn't stayed long, it had been interesting to see him hanging around the single women there. Havoc wasn't the type of guy to fawn over a woman, but the way he and Olivia had been verbally sparring was entertaining to say the least. He was the last guy Tyler expected to ever have a girlfriend, but hell. Anything was possible.

"That's good she went to bed without any trouble. Hopefully I wore her out a bit playing soccer earlier. She's a fierce little thing. I didn't expect a little girl to play so aggressively," he said with a chuckle. "I have to admit I was impressed. She can really hustle."

Rachel laughed, and he loved the light sound of it. She looked even more relaxed now, and he watched as she sank into the armchair near the sofa, her eyes twinkling as she looked over at him. Her clean, fresh scent filled the air around them. He wasn't even sure how to describe it—like fresh air and sunshine. Pure Rachel. He'd have loved if she sat right at his side, but he'd take this for now. Tyler didn't want her ever to feel uncomfortable around him, and this was the first time he'd ever been in her apartment.

"She's a competitive kid. I can't imagine where she got that from."

"Oh yeah?" he asked with a grin, watching as Rachel's lips quirked. "So, I should challenge you to something next time to see that competitive spirit in action? Hmmm. I'm going to have to think about this," he teased. "What kind of contest should we have?"

"None," she said, a pretty flush pinkening her cheeks.

Tyler resisted the urge to groan. He'd love to see her flush like that as he kissed her. Or, once he got to know her better, when he took her to bed. Tyler had no doubt he could spend hours exploring her body, finding different ways to pleasure her. Depending on how the evening went, maybe he could sneak in a goodbye kiss. He wasn't exactly about to make out on the sofa with her though or take her anywhere near a bed tonight.

"I don't know," he countered. "We could make our competition interesting. The winner has to cook the loser dinner."

"Dinner could work," Rachel said. "How good of a cook are you anyway?"

"What makes you think you'd win? I could go for a good meal," he teased. "We didn't even decide what we'd be playing, though."

"I have my ways of winning," she said, flipping her blonde hair back over her shoulder with a smug grin. Yep. Tyler was a goner. He'd probably let her win and deal with cooking dinner just to see that smile on her face again. He was competitive in many ways, too, but hell. It would be worth losing to see that cute flush spreading across her cheeks again and that sparkle in her blue eyes. Then again, maybe he should pick some sport she knew nothing about just so he could teach her. Then they'd be spending even more time together. Keira posed a bit of a challenge though, because no doubt she'd want to join in the fun.

"I'm sure you do," he murmured.

Their eyes locked for a beat, and then Rachel glanced away. "Can I get you something else to drink? If I'd planned on having you over, I'd have been more prepared."

"No worries," he assured her. "I'm good. You look less stressed than you did earlier this afternoon," he observed.

"Is it that obvious?" she asked with a laugh. "I'm just glad Keira's home. The good news is, she's not supposed to see her dad for another few weeks, although I've got a feeling he'll be asking the court for more visitation, especially given his new girlfriend. Anyway, I'm sure you want to talk about something else. Oh! I bought brownie mix earlier when I was at the grocery store. Want me to bake them for dessert? Keira can have some tomorrow."

"Sure, if you want, but don't feel obligated just because I'm here."

"It's fine. I planned to make them this weekend anyway. They're quick, and then we can hang out while they're in the oven."

She rose from the chair, and Tyler followed her into the kitchen. She ducked down to grab a large mixing bowl from a low cabinet, and he swore his cock twitched at the sight of her ass in those jeans again. Damn. She stood back up, and he realized she was slightly shorter now that she was barefoot. She looked sexy and pretty in that floral blouse, with her blonde hair trailing down her back. He had to resist the urge to go to her, gently pulling her into his arms. He'd love to know what her body felt like pressed up against his, but he could be good and simply get to know her better tonight.

Rachel moved efficiently around the kitchen, grabbing eggs from the fridge and vegetable oil from the cupboard.

"Can I help?" he asked.

"Sure," she said, handing him a pair of scissors. "Just cut the top off the mix and dump it into the bowl." She set about cracking the eggs, and Tyler did as she instructed. Before long, she was handing him the spoon. "Here you go. Just stir it all together."

"Okay. Are the eggs supposed to look like that?"

She glanced in the bowl, seeing the yolks he was referring to. "Yeah, just mix them right in. Haven't you ever made brownies before?"

"Honestly? No." He chuckled as she looked at him in disbelief. Tyler shrugged. "What can I say? If I need a dessert or something, I just pick it up at the grocery store. I can cook a few things, and grilling is pretty basic, but baking I've never actually attempted."

"Tyler, my five-year-old can mix brownies," she teased.

His lips quirked as he enjoyed this more playful side of Rachel. She'd let her guard down here in her own apartment, with her daughter safe and fast asleep. She was always friendly, but this was more— the real her.

"Are you making fun of my skills in the kitchen?" he asked with a wink. "I can do plenty of other things. I'm good with cars and weapons. Heavy artillery. But brownie mix? Clearly, it's beyond my area of expertise."

"Yeah, yeah, just mix it all right in. Put those muscles to good use," she joked, crossing over to preheat the oven.

He jokingly flexed for her before stirring the brownie batter, loving the way she actually giggled. "All right, let's see how you did," she said, coming to stand right beside him and setting the brownie pan on the counter. He stiffened slightly, resisting the urge to touch her. He could feel the heat from her body, smell her fresh scent. She was nothing but sunshine and pure goodness, and he loved how happy she made him feel. Just baking brownies together was fun, because she was at his side.

"Not bad for an amateur," she said, peering into the bowl.

"Not bad?" he scoffed, glancing over at her. "They look awesome. Good enough to eat."

"Ha, ha," she said, playfully elbowing him.

Unable to resist any longer, he caught her in his arms as she shrieked in surprise. "Now I'm putting my muscles to good use," he joked, swinging her up into the air.

She clung to him, laughing, as he held her close. "Don't drop me!"

"Drop you? You barely weigh anything," he laughed, spinning her around the kitchen once more before finally setting her back on her feet. He brushed some of the hair back from her face, smiling. She was so damn close to him but didn't back away. "God, you're pretty," he said.

"Tyler," she protested.

"Rachel."

"I haven't dated anyone in—forever. It feels like forever."

"So? Like I said earlier, it's not something you forget. I think we're doing just fine tonight, although I'm trying to resist the urge to kiss you."

Her gaze dropped to his mouth, and then she jumped slightly as the oven beeped. "It's preheated," she said breathlessly, glancing over to it and then looking back up at him.

A beat passed. "Okay. Show me what to do next." Tyler sensed that she was already feeling nervous. He'd love to kiss the hell out of her, but he could be patient. If the oven hadn't beeped right at that moment, he'd have moved in for a kiss. He could tell she'd have let him, too, but now her thoughts were holding her back. Tyler had loved holding her in his arms, moving with her around the kitchen. Someday he'd love to carry her like that straight to his bed. He'd love to kiss those pink lips, too, but he'd just missed his chance. He didn't want to frighten her. Tyler knew he needed to go slowly with Rachel. She searched his face but then turned her attention back to the food. He didn't miss the way she lightly bit her lip. Tyler wanted to reassure her, but she was already back to business. "Grab the bowl of batter. Let's finish baking these brownies."

# Chapter 5

Tyler grinned as he headed to the parking lot on base a few days later. His buddies had given him shit about the way he was always checking his phone for texts from Rachel over the past few days, but he didn't care. They'd hung out for hours on Saturday, watching a movie and eating the brownies they'd made. On Sunday, he'd already had plans with his friends, but when he'd gotten home and noticed Rachel and Keira outside, he'd headed right over to join them. Whereas in the past, he'd had qualms about intruding, now he felt nothing but comfortable jogging over.

Rachel had been happy to see him, and Keira had been thrilled to kick around a soccer ball once again.

"What's up with the shit-eating grin, man?" Mark "Mayhem" Covington asked as he caught up with Tyler. "Are you seeing your lady again tonight?"

"She's not my lady—yet. And yes, I am. Her

daughter has a gymnastics class later, and there's a coffee place next door. Rachel and I are going to grab coffee while Keira's in gymnastics."

"Sweet. I wasn't sure what was up when you guys left so quickly on Saturday, but I'm glad things are going well."

Tyler lifted a shoulder. "Yeah, I'd love to take her to dinner, but there's the whole babysitter thing. We'll figure it out. Last Saturday, we had to get home and meet her ex because he was dropping her daughter off early. Rachel actually offered to take a cab back to her place. Can you believe that? She didn't want me to miss the barbeque."

Mark chuckled. "She's a mom. She's used to taking care of other people."

"And you know that how?" Tyler asked, looking at him in disbelief.

"My older sister is married with kids. I've seen how it goes. She'll basically sacrifice everything for them."

Tyler shook his head. "My sister is younger and still in college. She's a blogger," he added, chuckling. "She wastes so much time posting pictures and crap on social media, I can't imagine her ever thinking about anything but herself. Apparently, her obsession with photographing her life works though. She's making decent money from basically doing nothing."

"Who is?" Brian "Blaze" Peterson asked as he caught up to them. He slung his gym bag over his shoulder, looking at Tyler curiously.

"My sister. Remember when I was showing you those photo ops she did?"

"Oh hell. Yeah, I remember. The cute blonde," he said, glancing over at Mark as if that explained everything.

Tyler elbowed him. "Hell, man. My sister is off limits. First of all, she's only twenty-two. Second, she's my sister."

"Third, she's way too pretty for your ugly ass," Mark joked.

"Wait, how do you know what she looks like?" Tyler asked in surprise.

Mark lifted a shoulder. "Blaze showed me the photos online," he said with a chuckle. "You have to admit, she's a looker. Not that we'd ever be disrespectful to your sister, man."

Tyler shook his head. "She gets all kinds of free stuff for posting on social media. We're in the wrong career. The Navy might give us hazard duty pay, but I don't doubt that she'll be making more money than me someday if she keeps this up."

Mark snorted. "Shit. I can't imagine spending my time doing stuff like that. It's so fake. I mean, I'm not knocking your sister, man. I know plenty of people are making money that way, but hell. It sounds exhausting."

"Yep. Almost as grueling as carrying a ninety-pound rucksack across the desert for a week straight, getting shot at by enemy fire."

"Point taken," Mark said. "I'm just not into the fake aspect of at all—snapping photos of everything you do. You're basically just showing people a highlight reel of your life."

"Well, you won't catch me doing that. It works for her though," Tyler said with a shrug. "As long as she's happy, it seems pretty harmless. She knows to be careful."

Mark frowned but didn't comment further. "I

guess you don't want to grab a beer with us tonight if you've got plans already?"

"Negative."

"What plans are these?" Brian asked. "Do you have a hot date or something?"

"Something. I'm having coffee with Rachel while her daughter's taking a class. No hot dates since we've got a kiddo in tow."

Brian chuckled. "Well, starting slow isn't all bad, but you already know the woman. At this rate, the kid will be in college before you can make a move."

Tyler muttered under his breath. "I'd love to take her to dinner, but like I was just telling Mark, there's the whole babysitting issue. I don't suppose you want to babysit Keira this weekend so I can take Rach on an actual date? How about you and Mark both, since he's such an expert on children and you're so concerned about my love life?"

"No way," Mark immediately said with a laugh. "I've got a niece and nephew, but I'm just the cool uncle. I'm good with that. I appreciate you thinking of me though."

"That'd be a hell no from me," Brian said.

"I figured as much. Well, my sister's coming into town in a few weeks. Maybe I can talk her into babysitting duty, assuming we're not out on an op. She's doing some kind of photo shoot down on the pier, but she won't be busy every second. It'd be up to Rachel of course."

"Now that, I might volunteer to help with," Mark said, scrubbing a hand over his jaw. "I'd love to see your sister trying to keep up with a young kid. What if a hair got out of place or something?"

"Don't be an ass," Tyler said.

"You're so laid back, it's hard to imagine she's the total opposite. Make sure you introduce us to her when she's in town. We need to meet this Instagram famous sister of yours."

"She's not famous. She definitely has a hell of a lot of followers though. I'm still not sure how she did it. In our line of work, we try to stay under the radar. She's sharing her whole live on social media," he said, shaking his head.

The men said their goodbyes. Mark and Brian walked over to their own vehicles, talking about what bar they were meeting up at. Ace was heading home to his woman, but it sounded like Havoc and Rob might meet up with the others. No doubt those two would've been happier if Ace and Addison joined them—then at least there was a chance her friends would come along. Havoc would never admit he was interested in Olivia, but Tyler had heard Rob asking about Cassie. He wasn't sure what the story was there. He didn't have time to worry about it right now though. He needed to get home, change out of his uniform, and then head out with Rachel and her daughter. He couldn't wait to spend some time alone together, even if they only had an hour tonight.

\*\*\*

"Bye! See you later, sweetie!" Rachel said, waving goodbye to Keira. She pulled open the door of the gymnastics studio and headed outside, where Tyler was patiently waiting for her on the sidewalk. He looked handsome as hell in jeans and a polo shirt. No doubt he'd changed after work, but even dressed casually, he looked good.

She walked up to him, smiling. Tyler smelled faintly of soap and cologne, and she loved that he'd taken time to get ready for their coffee date, casual as though it was. The last time she'd seen him, they'd been running around outside kicking a soccer ball with Keira, getting all sweaty. She loved the outdoors and spending time with her daughter, but it was nice doing something quieter, too. If she got to sit close to Tyler while they enjoyed coffee together, all the better.

"Keira seemed excited," he commented as they walked toward the coffee place.

"She is, but she loves just about everything. As you probably noticed, she's got a ton of energy."

"You don't say," Tyler joked.

She playfully elbowed him, smiling as she caught the expression on his face. The light gray shirt he had on set off his pale blue eyes, and she loved how he was focused totally on her. She swore she could get lost staring into those eyes. Her cheeks heated, and she looked away. She didn't need to trip over her own two feet as they walked next door.

Still, Tyler had to realize he was a good-looking man. Why he'd be interested in a busy mom like her defied belief. They were both fairly young. Plenty of moms at Keira's school were a good decade older than her. Tyler wasn't tied down the way she was. She loved her daughter more than anything, and although she was attracted to Tyler, she needed to be cautious. Sneaking in a coffee date here or there was fun, but soon he'd realize her schedule wasn't her own.

What then?

He'd probably move on to someone more available. When you were used to having your evenings and weekends free, suddenly having a child to care for would be a shock to anyone. She wouldn't blame him if he'd prefer someone with more freedom in their life. It would sting to see him with another woman, but she'd have to be patient and see what happened. Give Tyler the benefit of the doubt. Rachel hadn't even dated in years, so there was no sense in pining away now for something she'd probably never have.

"Coffee is on me," Tyler said as he pulled open the door to the cute little coffee shop.

"What? No way. You drove us over here and even installed the extra booster seat in the backseat of your truck for Keira. The least I can do is pay."

"There's no way I'm letting you buy me coffee," Tyler said in a low voice. "Call it sexist or whatever you want, but this counts as a date. I'm not letting you pay for me. And when I eventually take you to dinner, I'm paying, too. Just letting you know in advance," he said with a wink.

"Tyler," she protested.

"Now, what can I get you?" he asked, effectively ending any discussion on the matter. His blue eyes were sparkling in amusement, and she could see he was pleased with himself. It was cute that he was so insistent on buying her coffee, but goodness. She was used to handling everything in her life on her own.

"Fine. You can pay today, but I'm making no promises for the future. And, I think I'll get a chai latte."

"Are those good?"

She giggled. "Well, I wouldn't order it if it was bad, now would I?"

"Touché," he said with a chuckle. "I'll stick with a

regular latte. Honestly, compared to the awful black coffee they have on base, I'm sure anything here is good though."

"Beggars can't be choosers, right?"

"Exactly."

"I practically inhaled the stuff when Keira was a baby. I'd have a pot of black coffee on every day. Those nights were exhausting."

"I'm sorry," he said, glancing over at her. "That must have been rough. It makes me dislike your ex even more for putting all that on you. It's a dick move to abandon your child like that—to have abandoned you as well. I'll be nice when I meet the guy, but hell. I'd love to give him a piece of my mind."

"You know he didn't even ask about you the other day when he dropped her off? I thought he'd be curious about who you were or why you were at my apartment. But nope, not a single word."

The woman in front of them ordered her drink, and she and Tyler stepped up to the counter. He placed their order and paid, then shocked her by taking her hand, gently tugging her over to wait for their drinks. She appreciated that he was angry at Kyle on her behalf, but even more, she liked the fact that he had no qualms about showing her that he was interested in her. She smiled up at him, loving the feel of his strong fingers wrapped around hers. It felt like they were a couple. Obviously, they weren't any such thing. It was a quick date at that. But it felt good to be standing there at Tyler's side.

She could tell that Tyler was the type of man who liked to take charge. It certainly wasn't in an overbearing way, but he had no problem handling situations as they arose. No doubt if Kyle starting giving her more trouble about custody, Tyler would be in her corner. And even though holding hands right now was a small gesture, she loved having that connection between them.

Goosebumps prickled her skin as they stood there. Tyler's cologne was yummy. Normally, she wasn't really into cologne on men, but his wasn't at all overpowering. Something about the scent of him drew her right in. Plus, the feeling of his tall, broad body at her side made her feel safe. His thumb skimmed over the back of her hand, and she edged slightly closer to him, enjoying his strength and warmth.

"The guys were giving me grief earlier," he admitted, his eyes sparking with amusement. "I think they're just jealous because they're single, hitting up a bar tonight, and I asked you out."

"Well, from the brief time we were at the barbeque, some of them had no trouble flirting with the women there. That one guy—Havoc? He seemed to be laying it on thick."

"Tell me about it. He has no trouble wooing the ladies, but he's not really a relationship kind of guy. I can see the rest of them settling down—eventually. Ace certainly seems happy with Addison. They started dating not too long ago, and she's already moved in with him." The barista called Tyler's name, indicating their drinks were ready, and they walked to the counter, hand-in-hand.

It was hard to imagine ever living with a man. She'd had a boyfriend in college, but they'd each lived with roommates. Then she dated a bit when she was younger, falling for Kyle. It was odd how the man himself was a major mistake, yet Keira was the best thing that had ever happened to her.

Rachel took a sip of her chai latte, holding it as Tyler led her to a cozy table in the back. He released her hand but surprised her again by pulling out a chair for her to sit down. This wasn't some fancy restaurant. It was just a coffee date. Still, she loved how sweet he was to her. She was used to looking after her daughter, but having someone else pay close attention to her made her heartbeat speed up. Tyler was attentive and all too aware of everything going on. Briefly, she wondered what kissing him would be like. Having him make love to her. No doubt he'd pay close attention, noticing what she liked.

He pulled his chair closer to hers and sat down. It was cozy. Intimate. It felt like they were in their own little world, sitting close at the small table. The coffee shop was fairly quiet right now, partly because it was dinner time. They could've grabbed a quick bite, but she'd still have to feed her daughter. This was perfect. And warmth flooded through her at the idea that Tyler wanted to spend any time together. Obviously, the night wasn't going to end with her in his bed—or vice versa. They both knew she had Keira to look after.

Her cheeks flushed at the idea of her and Tyler beneath the sheets. He was in perfect shape— muscular and strong. He seemed to enjoy being in control. Would he act that way in bed, too? She didn't want an aggressive lover, but he seemed the perfect amount of take-charge, yet considerate. That was just his personality.

"Is your chai latte good?" he asked.

"Perfect," she assured him. "I've tried making them at home before, but it's just not the same. They have those mixes to use, but it never tastes right."

"As long as you're enjoying it," he said with a grin, taking a sip of his own drink.

Briefly, she wondered what he'd do if she complained. Rachel was fairly down-to-earth, with not much fazing her, but he'd probably get her another drink, no questions asked if something was wrong. It was a little surprising how attentive he was. She liked that he noticed the small things though. He'd brought her flowers the day of the barbeque. He'd driven her straight home when she needed to get back, taking everything in stride. Hopefully he wasn't too good to be true.

"What are you thinking so hard about?" he asked, his lips quirking.

"Honestly?"

Tyler laughed. "Absolutely."

"I'm kind of wondering if you're too good to be true," she admitted. "I know we're just getting to know one another better, but geez. You're practically perfect."

"I'm not perfect—just ask my teammates. But I'd never be a jackass either. If for some reason things didn't work out between us, I can be an adult about it. We live next door to each other, which could be awkward. I'd never do something to make you or Keira uncomfortable though."

"See? That's what I mean. You say sweet things like that, and it's almost too good to be true."

Tyler set his cup down and nailed her with a gaze. "There's no nice way to say this, so I'll just blurt it right out. Your ex was a dick. I wouldn't do that to a woman—ever. I'd never abandon my child. I'd never abandon the mother of my child. If things got serious between us one day, I'd be there for both you and Keira. That's how relationships work. And I would like to see more of you—to see if this connection we have goes somewhere."

"I want to see more of you, too, it's just—"

"I know. It's difficult with a five-year-old, and I get that. We'll figure something out. My sister will be in town in a few weeks. She'd be happy to babysit Keira so I could take you out to dinner if you'd be comfortable with that. I know you said your regular babysitter went to college."

"I miss her all the time," Rachel said with a small laugh. "I can't even run an errand alone."

"I can watch Keira if you ever need me to."

Her eyes widened.

"Don't look so shocked," he said with a chuckle. "If you've got something to do, I wouldn't mind. I'm in and out on the weekends, but just let me know. By the way, you look pretty tonight."

She flushed, watching with interest as Tyler took her hand. His thick fingers wove between hers, and she could see the veins and tendons. For a flash, she imagined them moving all over her body—sliding under her bra strap, caressing her breasts, touching that tender area between her thighs. Tyler was masculine and quite good-looking. Her heart raced just being close to him, but it was his personality that truly made her melt.

"Thank you," she said, knowing her face was probably still red. "You look nice, too."

"I figured I better change out of the fatigues."

"I don't know," she teased. "There's something to be said for a man in uniform."

"Noted," he quipped. "And just so you know, if

we don't get to spend much time alone together because of the whole childcare situation, I'm fine with that, too. I can hang with you and Keira. Maybe we can snuggle up on the sofa after her bedtime," Tyler added with a wink.

"I'm just…not used to this."

"I know. I would've asked you out when you first moved in, but like I said, I thought you were with Kyle."

"You really wanted to ask me out then," she said, smiling.

"Of course. You're smart, pretty, funny. Should I go on?" he teased. "I could tell you were a nice person, even if we didn't talk too much at first. And yes, I was attracted to you, in case that wasn't obvious."

Her phone buzzed with a text, and she reluctantly pulled her hand free from Tyler's. "I better check that, just in case."

"Of course."

She pulled her phone from her purse, frowning at the message.

*My lawyer is filing with the court tomorrow regarding my visitation schedule. I deserve more time with Keira. That's my right as her father.*

Rachel froze, blinking, as she stared at the text. Several more texts quickly followed.

*I'm letting you know as a courtesy.*

*No doubt they'll grant me more time.*

*Since I brought her home early last weekend, I'd like Keira to have dinner with me on Saturday.*

"What's wrong? Is Keira okay?" Tyler asked. He'd stiffened, and she could see he was ready to rush next door if there was a problem at the gymnastics studio.

She let out a breath. "Keira's fine. That was Kyle. He'll be petitioning the court for more time with Keira. His lawyer is filing tomorrow. I figured it was coming. He used to see her for only a few hours a month, and then he got an entire day. We've been arguing about it recently, and I told him we had to abide by the court order. Now he's officially requesting additional time," she said, tears smarting her eyes.

"Hey," Tyler said, taking her hand and lightly rubbing his thumb over the back of it. "It'll be okay. You have a lawyer, too, right? You can tell them he was an absentee father for what—four, five years? They're not going to let him get custody or anything. Maybe he'll get a little extra time with Keira, but you can fight back."

"He wants to see her on Saturday for dinner," she whispered. "Sorry," she said, quickly swiping away her tears. "I'm just frustrated. They were supposed to have dinner last weekend, as you remember, and that didn't work out at all."

"Does Keira like spending time with him? Aside from the sushi mishap, which was dumb on his part. Does she usually enjoy it?"

"Not especially, but she's getting used to it. The first few times she went, she cried and cried. It was a supervised visitation, but that didn't make me feel any better. Now he's allowed to take her for an entire day. He's got a large house with a swing set and trampoline he had installed in the backyard. She's got an entire room full of toys there. He's totally trying to buy her love, and it sucks, especially since he seems more worried about impressing his girlfriend than caring for a child. But what if she likes it there better?"

"She loves you, Rach. Anyone can see that. Sure, maybe Kyle can afford to buy fancy shit for her, but none of that makes up for you caring for her since the day she was born. You just said yourself that she doesn't especially like seeing him."

"I did, didn't I?" she mused, glancing back up at Tyler. She hated the concerned look on his face. She was a strong, independent woman. A mother. She didn't need to sit here falling apart. Plus, they only had a little while before they had to get her daughter. Keira would be able to tell if she was upset. "I just wish he didn't seem more worried about Carly than his own daughter."

"What's the deal with that anyway? It's a new relationship?"

"Sort of. I'm not actually even sure where he met her. He's a musician and probably dated a lot over the years. I mean, shoot, I fell for him years ago. You know the story with that. Now suddenly, out of nowhere, he pops back into my life and wants to see his daughter. He had been paying child support, but we only communicated through our lawyers and the courts. He had absolutely zero interest in meeting Keira."

"It seems a little odd. You'd think in a new relationship, you'd appreciate being free to date without a child around. Not that I'm complaining," he said, looking at her seriously. "I'm just surprised he'd try to get visitation rights after years had gone by right when he started dating someone new. The timing seems a little off."

"It does. I thought he was just trying to impress her—show Carly he could be a good dad or whatever.

Maybe she wants kids someday." She looked down at her chai latte. "I'm not sure about Saturday either. I don't want to send her to dinner but maybe I should."

"I'll support you with whatever you decide to do. If he's going to petition the courts anyway, maybe seeing Keira two weeks in a row isn't a bad thing. It'll give her a chance to get to know him better, right? A couple of hours will be over before you know it."

"Yeah. I know. The courts will side with him, saying he has a right to see his own child. I get that, but this situation just sucks. We're not parents who got divorced with kids who were used to seeing both of us every night. She barely knows him. Now he suddenly wants to be an involved father?"

She blew out a sigh and thumbed a text into her phone.

*I'll get back to you about Saturday.*

It buzzed with a response.

*Let me know soonest.*

Frowning, she brushed her hair back from her face. Tyler's gaze tracked her movements, and she could tell he was worried about her. "Ready to get Keira?" he asked softly.

"Yeah. We should head over."

"He's acted like a dick, Rach. We both know that. Maybe he's had a change of heart over the years and really wants to be more involved. You can try fighting him in court."

Rachel shrugged helplessly. "Maybe. I don't have much choice but to see how it plays out. I don't doubt that the courts will grant him additional time with her. I've got nothing to use against him at this point, so I'll just have to deal with it somehow." She glanced at her phone. "Class is almost over, so let's go."

They stood, and Tyler wrapped his arm around her shoulders, pulling her close as they walked to the door. She felt safe feeling the weight of his muscular arm draped around her. Their date had completely flipped from fun to somber, with Kyle's texts putting a damper on the evening. She was quiet as they walked across the coffee shop, and Tyler surprised her by ducking and softly kissing her temple. "We'll figure this out, Rach." He kissed her lightly once more, as if unable to resist, and then pulled open the door to the coffee shop.

The balmy San Diego air soothed her as they walked out, and she was relieved to have Tyler at her side. He steadied her somehow, even though she was used to standing on her own two feet. It was humbling to realize she needed someone in her corner—that she didn't have to do everything all alone. Yes, she would've put one foot in front of the other and walked over to get her daughter if Tyler hadn't been here, but having his support meant everything.

Things weren't exactly serious between her and Tyler yet. How could they be? They'd only recently even considered the idea of dating. She knew she could trust him though. She was attracted to him, and the feeling seemed to be mutual. Life was just easier with him around. More exciting. Neither of them knew where things would go, but she had a good feeling about the man at her side.

"Is Keira going to be upset I have my arm around you?" he suddenly asked.

Rachel looked up at him, touched that he'd even worry about that. Kyle had no problems introducing her daughter to Carly. Who knew if they held hands or kissed in front of Keira? Tyler was considerate though. Whereas Kyle often seemed more concerned about his girlfriend, Tyler worried about them both. She loved that about him.

"No, she likes you," Rachel admitted. Her thoughts wandered as Tyler pulled open the door of the gymnastics studio. Her daughter did like him. Granted, she didn't send Keira off alone with Tyler for an entire day like she had to with Kyle, but she had a feeling Keira wouldn't be too upset. Tyler was a good guy. Kids seemed to sense that about adults, and her own gut feeling told her they were safe with Tyler, too. It just made her wonder all that much more about her ex and what his intentions really were.

# Chapter 6

Tyler leaned back in his chair in the bullpen Friday afternoon, glancing around at his teammates. Their commanding officer, Commander Slate Hutchinson, had just called a last-minute briefing. The team had been monitoring multiple situations around the world during the past few weeks, so it wasn't exactly surprising that they might get sent out soon. He'd made plans to see Rachel tomorrow though, since her daughter would be over at Kyle's, and it sucked that he might have to cancel.

"Any idea what this is about?" Tyler asked, glancing over at Rob.

"Negative. It could be a number of things. Somalia. That missing boat in the South Pacific. I'm guessing the Pentagon wants us to move in on the Moheed Kalmati terror cell gaining strength in Pakistan though. Shit isn't exactly going to calm down in Africa anytime soon. And the missing boat?" He lifted a shoulder. "Possible, but I don't know. I don't think we have any new intelligence on that."

"Shit. Ever since the withdrawal of U.S. troops from Afghanistan, more groups in the Middle East seem to be springing up and gaining strength. What a clusterfuck."

"They were there before," Rob noted dryly.

"Yeah, but these groups are more aggressive now. All the attacks occurring over there? Hell. It's a never-ending cycle."

Ace came walking in, his face unreadable. "The CO will be here soon," he said, pulling out a chair and sinking down. "I just had a quick briefing with him."

"What's the word, Ace?" Havoc asked, scrubbing a hand over his short beard. "Are we go for an op?"

"It looks like we'll be flying to the Middle East in the morning," Ace confirmed. "We'll probably be sent in right along the Af-Pak border."

"Shit," Tyler muttered. All eyes swung to him. "I finally had an actual date planned with Rachel this weekend. Not that I don't want to get those bastards behind all the attacks in Pakistan, but the timing is bad."

"That sucks, man. Rachel is cute," Rob said.

"As cute as Cassie?" Havoc asked, snickering as he crossed his arms and leaned back in his seat.

Rob nailed him with a glare but didn't answer as Ace muttered a curse. "Addison's worried about her. Ever since Addison was kidnapped, Cassie's been more withdrawn."

"She was scared as hell the day I drove her home," Rob admitted. "Olivia made it sound like Cassie was usually friendly and bubbly, but she seems skittish to me. I know she was scared that afternoon, but it's more than that. She seemed afraid I'd hurt her or something—not that I'd ever fucking harm a woman."

Brian lifted a shoulder. "Maybe she's just not into you, man."

"I didn't ask her out," Rob said, nailing him with a glare. "I drove her home after Addison was kidnapped right from the damn restaurant parking lot. I don't blame her for being frightened about that."

Tyler frowned, recalling the incident. Addison had confided in Ace about some suspicions she had regarding her roommate. It turned out, her roommate Matt was involved in a sex-trafficking ring, and when the leader thought Addison knew too much about it, he'd kidnapped her in an attempt to cover up his wrongdoings. He'd blackmailed her and then had been planning to rape her in a hotel room until Ace and the team had rushed in. He knew Ace was still pissed as hell at the man behind it all. That guy was in jail now, and Matt had been killed.

Addison was safe, but none of them would soon forget the incident. Tyler didn't know Cassie. He didn't even know Addison all that well yet either. She'd only recently gotten together with his SEAL team leader.

"We should get all the women together," Ace said. "I know Addison wants to get to know Rachel. It'd be nice for all of them to connect with each other while we're gone. The girls on Raptor's team are all close," he said, referring to Blake "Raptor" Reynolds, the leader of the other SEAL team on base. "I'll get Rachel's number from you to give Addison." His gaze shifted to Rob.

"I'm not dating Cassie," Rob said. "I just drove

her home one day."

"I am dating Rachel, but hell," Tyler said, shaking his head. "It's all still new. I know she's not seeing anyone else, but we're not exactly a couple yet."

"With 'yet' being the operative word," Havoc said with a smirk. "We can all see that she has you wrapped around her finger."

Any further discussion ended as their CO stormed into the room, looking irritated. "Gentlemen," he said, briefly looking at the men seated around the table before crossing toward the massive TV screen at the front of the room. "We've got a secure video conference with the Pentagon. They have new information on the Moheed Kalmati terror group in Pakistan."

Admiral Brown's image suddenly appeared on the giant screen, and he began to address the men assembled in the bullpen. Tyler knew the admiral was attending several events in Washington this week. No doubt he'd scheduled briefings at the Pentagon while he was in town. "I just briefed Commander Hutchinson moments ago. State has intelligence indicating that several Americans are being held hostage in Pakistan by the Kalmati terror group. They never returned to the U.S. Embassy, and one Marine Embassy Guard was shot. He's in surgery and will hopefully be able to provide a statement when he wakes up."

"Shit," Tyler muttered under his breath. Tensions had been increasing in Pakistan recently—as had the frequency of attacks on Westerners there.

"I just got confirmation that there are five civilians missing," Admiral Brown said. "As you may be aware, I'm in Washington this week for several events. I was given this information directly from the State Department. The rest of the intelligence community will be aware of the matter soon."

"Are these embassy employees, sir?" Ace asked. "State Department?"

"Four of them are. The other is a DOD contractor—former military. He's combat trained, but the rest are civilians. One woman is diabetic and in need of insulin. Commander Hutchinson will provide the details of the operation. The group is not believed to be in Islamabad anymore. As you may be aware, they've got a camp near the Af-Pak border, which is where the Americans are being held. State is pressing the urgency of this matter given the medical condition of one of the women. Moheed Kalmati has not been located yet. This is strictly a rescue mission. Your team will retrieve the hostages and escort them back to U.S. soil. Dismissed."

His image disappeared from the secure connection, and Commander Hutchinson faced the room. "This mission has been a clusterfuck since before it even began. Someone over in Islamabad wasn't doing their job. The threats were increasing to the Embassy, and yet these employees were allowed to travel with only a single contractor for security."

"Jesus. What time are we moving in, sir?" Ace asked.

"Wheels up at oh-five-hundred. I know you weren't planning to brief and pack on a Friday night, but duty calls."

Their CO crossed to a laptop, pulling up maps that appeared on the giant TV screen. It was going to be a long night, and Tyler still had to get in touch with

Rachel at some point and cancel their plans for tomorrow.

***

"I can't believe we got ice cream so late at night!" Keira shrieked happily, racing down the sidewalk bordering the parking lot. Rachel hurried to keep up with her daughter, already regretting the decision. It would be tough to get her down to bed tonight with all that sugar she'd just consumed. She'd wanted to do something fun before she had to send her daughter off tomorrow afternoon and evening with Kyle though. They'd eaten dinner at the apartment, and she'd suddenly had the urge to take her daughter for ice cream.

She loved doing spontaneous things with her and hated that a different visitation schedule could eventually prevent that. Kyle hadn't mentioned wanting partial custody, but she was concerned. Maybe she should've had him relinquish his parental rights at Keira's birth. She couldn't have collected child support, but then she wouldn't be dealing with sending her daughter off with a stranger either.

Tyler hadn't been home yet when they'd left. The other evening, he'd mentioned how his buddies were out at a bar. Was that where he was tonight? Not that he owed her an explanation. He was a single guy. They were dating, not officially a couple. She was a parent. It had been years since she'd gone out for a carefree Friday night. She couldn't fault him for hanging out with his friends, but she could admit she felt the tiniest twinge of jealousy at the freedom he had.

People without young kids had no idea what it was like to be a parent 24/7. She loved her daughter more than anything, but a carefree night out was almost a fantasy. Hopefully no other women were hitting on Tyler if he was out with his friends, but who was she kidding? Tyler was cute as hell. Handsome, but not in an intimidating way like some men. She knew some women loved the gruff, masculine look, but she appreciated his more boyish charm. Tyler made her feel comfortable and safe. He made her heart race, too, but that was an entirely different matter.

"Ice cream tonight was a special treat," Rachel told her daughter. "It's almost bedtime though, so get out all of your energy now. We have to settle down when we go inside."

"Let's go to the playground!" Keira yelled.

Rachel paused. It wasn't a bad idea. Ten minutes of running around would burn off some of that energy she seemed to have. She agreed, following her daughter as they turned and headed the other way. Keira was already laughing with happiness, thinking she'd gotten away with something.

Rachel's phone buzzed, and she stiffened. Kyle had already texted her several times today. She hoped it wasn't him again but pulled her phone out of her purse, frowning.

I assume your lawyer will look over the papers?

We haven't gotten a response from you yet. I'll take this to the judge, Rachel.

Blowing out a shaky sigh, she hurried after Keira. Maybe she should appreciate that Kyle was trying to amend the agreement through their lawyers, but damn. The man had been gone for years. What made him want to suddenly spend so much time with

Keira?

Rachel knew he wanted to impress his girlfriend, but geez. You'd think another woman wouldn't want to be bothered having her boyfriend's young child around.

Uneasiness washed over her, and she texted Kyle back.

My lawyer will get back to you next week.

Her phone buzzed one more time.

I'll be there tomorrow at three to get Keira. You can't keep me from my child.

Tears smarted her eyes, and she hurried to the playground. She quickly swiped a tear away before Keira noticed and suddenly heard Tyler calling out hello to them. Turning in surprise, she saw him jogging toward them in his fatigues. She assumed he hadn't gone to a bar dressed in his uniform, so maybe he'd been stuck working late. He was clutching a bag of food in his hand, so that meant he hadn't even eaten yet either, despite how late it now was.

"Hey, how are my favorite ladies?" he asked with a grin as he walked up. "What's wrong?" he asked, immediately noticing her distress as he got closer. He put his backpack and bag of food on the ground before moving toward her.

"Just problems with Kyle. He's being a jerk about the visitation schedule," she said in a low voice. "I'm just glad we have plans for tomorrow after he comes by to get Keira. I'm already stressed about…"

Tyler was frowning, and her stomach dropped. His jaw was clenched, and she could see the worry in his eyes. "You have to cancel for tomorrow."

He nodded, looking chagrined. "We're getting sent out on a mission. I've got to pack tonight and leave bright and early. We've been briefing for hours with our CO."

A tear slipped down her cheek as she tried to blink the wetness in her eyes away, and he immediately snaked an arm around her waist, pulling her close. "I'm sorry, Rach. I know you're stressed about everything with Kyle. I hate that I have to leave. I was looking forward to our date."

She let her forehead rest against his shoulder, sniffling slightly as his hand went to cup the back of her head. Tyler's lips pressed against her hair, and she wanted to melt right into him. Keira was probably about two seconds away from noticing she was upset. Tyler had just gotten home and had his own things to do before he left. She needed to pull herself together.

"I'm okay," she said quietly.

"You're not," he countered. "I'm sorry, baby." His hand shifted down to her neck, his thumb running back and forth across her skin. A shiver snaked down her spine. Tyler was muscular and strong, and the way he held her to him made her feel safe. Cared for. His muscled arm around her waist felt good as he held her close. She loved the way he held her pressed up right against him, leaving no doubt that he wanted her.

And when he'd just called her baby? She wanted to melt.

"Mommy, what's wrong?" Keira suddenly asked, rushing over.

"Nothing, sweetie, I'm fine," she said, pulling back and swiping away her tears.

"I haven't eaten dinner yet," Tyler said. "What do you say I hang out with you guys for a little while?" His eyes met hers. He looked unhappy that she was upset.

"Yes!" Keira said. "Can we play soccer?"

"No, honey, it's late. Maybe Tyler can come back to our apartment. He can eat while I get you ready for bed. Then he has some things to get done."

"Oh man," she pouted. "That's not fair."

"We'll play soccer when I get back, kiddo," Tyler said.

"Do you promise? Mr. Kyle hates soccer. I'd rather stay here with you and mom on those days. Plus, sushi looks gross. I liked the pizza you got us."

Rachel's heart tightened. Tyler was still watching her and then glanced back at her daughter. "I promise, kiddo."

He ducked down to grab his backpack and food, his eyes lingering on Rachel. She knew he was making sure she was okay. Tyler had his own stuff to worry about though. She didn't want him distracted on his mission wondering if she was okay. He had lots of things to do tonight as well. They might not have been dating before, but she was used to his leaving. Tyler needed to get things organized at his place, pack, and hopefully get some sleep if he was leaving early in the morning.

His frequent deployments had never bothered her before. He was just her neighbor. Now, it just made her feel sad. She'd miss him and was already starting to care about him, as fast as it seemed. He wasn't her boyfriend though, so she'd just have to pull herself together. Even if they were an actual couple, he'd still have to go. His job was with the Navy. If they were in a relationship, she'd just have to deal with it. Tyler loved his career and no doubt was good at what he did. She knew not just anyone could be a Navy

SEAL.

Looking over at Keira and Tyler, she forced herself to smile. Tomorrow evening, her daughter would be at her father's. She needed to enjoy the rest of tonight while both Keira and Tyler were here. "Come on. I'll race you guys to the sidewalk."

Keira immediately took off running, and she heard Tyler laughing behind them as she began running as well. No doubt he could easily catch them, but his deep laughter had her belly doing flips. She heard him running up behind her, and then Tyler was lifting her off the ground, his muscular arms wrapping around her as she shrieked in surprise.

He set her back down, turning her around but not letting her go. "I win," he said huskily, holding her close as Keira raced to the sidewalk, shrieking in excitement.

"I won! I won!" Keira shouted.

Tyler's heated gaze held hers. "I guess you did, Keira."

Rachel smiled up at him, suddenly happier than she'd been moments before. She loved Tyler's arms around her, and the intense way he was looking at her made her heart race. She quickly glanced over at her daughter. "Yeah, it looks like you won. Let's go upstairs," she said.

Keira raced ahead as Rachel looked back up at Tyler. "You cheated," she mock complained.

"I got what I wanted," he said with an easy grin. One hand moved to her face, cupping her cheek, and then he ducked down and kissed her softly. She gasped in surprise, the kiss over as soon as it had begun. Keira was waiting for them.

"I guess we should go upstairs."

His eyes blazed with intensity as he looked at her. "Lead the way," he murmured.

# Chapter 7

"I want to give you the names and cell numbers of some people, so you'll have them while I'm gone," Tyler said later that night. He'd eaten dinner and then gone back to his place to pack while Rachel tucked in her daughter. It sucked that he was leaving in the morning, but she had to admit it was nice that he lived right next door. He'd gotten packed but had come back when he was done. Now they had a little time alone together before they had to say goodbye.

How many times had they said goodbye before his other deployments? Of course, she'd worried about him then, in the way you did about your friends and neighbors. This was different tonight, and they both knew it.

Rachel and Tyler hadn't even officially established themselves as a couple, but here he was, hanging out with her before he had to go. In a way, she knew him so well, just from being neighbors. She knew his routine and how he'd still be in a good mood even after a hard day at work. She didn't know his favorite food or TV show or even his favorite football team. It was almost scary how much she'd already grown to care about him though.

"Names of who?" she asked.

She grabbed them each a bottle of water from the fridge and handed Tyler one. He twisted the cap and took a long pull, then set it on the counter. He'd brought some of his food over since it would just spoil while he was gone. He'd done it a couple of times in the past, but it just felt sad now. Like she'd have reminders that he wasn't here.

Tyler would be busy chasing down the bad guys or rescuing people or whatever his SEAL team did. She knew he couldn't tell her. She'd be here with her daughter, knowing his apartment was empty.

"Just some of the guys on the other team. I know you're stressed about Kyle, and if he's pressuring you about anything, give them a call. They can help handle him if needed while I'm gone."

"I can deal with Kyle," she said, rubbing her temples.

"I know, but you shouldn't have to do it all alone. Come here," Tyler said, pulling her to him. He guided her into the living room and plopped down on her sofa, tugging Rachel right into his lap as she giggled.

"What are you doing?" she asked with a smile.

"Giving you a hug." His arms wrapped more tightly around her, and she relaxed against him.

"I thought men didn't like to cuddle," she teased, contentedly snuggling further into him. He smelled faintly of his outdoorsy scent. Maybe it was the soap he used or else just pure Tyler. Either way, it was both comforting and sexy. She loved his scent and wanted to burrow right into him. She kind of wanted to strip him down and kiss him everywhere, too, she thought with a flush. It was far too soon for that. She wouldn't jump into bed too quickly with a man ever again. She'd been young and foolish when she was dating Kyle. And although she was attracted to Tyler, she wasn't going to let him see her naked yet. She trusted him, but she needed to take things more slowly than she had when she was young.

Tyler nuzzled the top of her head, seeming to enjoy holding her close as well. "Who told you that? If cuddling means I get to hold you in my arms, I'm all for it."

He shifted slightly, she could feel his muscular thighs beneath her. The man was nothing but pure athleticism and power, but she loved how careful he was with her. Even though she was taller than average for a woman, she felt small in his arms. Tyler trained hard, and she appreciated his muscles and strength. More than once, she'd wondered what it would feel like having Tyler move over her—inside of her.

Would they get to that point in their relationship? Or would his deployments and her busy life as a single mom prevent anything more serious from ever happening?

Tyler's lips lightly brushed against the top of her head. "I cancelled our dinner reservations for tomorrow. When I get back, I'm taking you out. We still haven't had a proper first date yet, although I love that you're comfortable enough with me to let me hold you like this."

"I like it, too," she admitted. She tilted her head up, meeting his gaze. "Do you know how long you'll be gone?"

"No," he said softly. "Even if I did, I wouldn't be able to tell you."

"I understand. I wish you didn't have to go," she said with a small sigh.

His large hand came up to her face, and he gently cupped her cheek. His thumb lightly trailed over her skin. "Me either, Rach. I always hear the guys on the other team complaining about leaving their women behind, and I didn't totally get it. I never had someone back home to worry about before. I care about you," he said, his voice gruff. "I know we haven't been dating long, but I've known you and Keira for almost a year. I'll worry about you when I'm gone."

"I'll worry about you, too. You're the one going somewhere dangerous."

Their eyes locked for a beat, and then Tyler was ducking his head. Her lips parted slightly, her heart pounding, and in the next moment, he was kissing her. It was soft and gentle at first, his full lips moving against hers as his hand slid to cradle the back of her head. She clutched onto him, and then the kiss quickly intensified.

Rachel shifted on his lap, feeling Tyler's arousal. He wanted her. She wasn't going to sleep with him tonight, but for the first time in years, she actually wanted to have sex. She was attracted to Tyler. She hadn't been with a man since having a baby, but her body responded to him in a way she couldn't control. Her nipples tightened as her breasts swelled, and arousal dampened her panties. She let out a tiny gasp as Tyler lifted her so that she was straddling him, and then he pressed her back into the sofa. Her hands landed on his broad shoulders, and she was pinned beneath him, flushed and aroused as her legs wound around his waist. She could feel his erection nestled against her core, and her heart raced.

She wasn't sure if she wanted to pull him closer or push him away. She wanted him so much it scared her. And she could see the desire in his eyes as well. "You're gorgeous, Rach," he murmured, moving to kiss the side of her neck. She arched up into him, gasping.

"Tyler," she whimpered.

He kissed her neck again, softly. "God, I don't want to stop, but we need to," he said, lightly nipping at the sensitive skin behind her ear. "I'm leaving tomorrow, and it's too soon right now anyway."

He lifted his head and kissed her tenderly. It was soft and sweet, and she clung to him as tears suddenly smarted her eyes. "I just don't want you to go. I hate that you're leaving."

"Don't cry, baby," he said, his voice thick with emotion. His intense gaze met hers, and she hated that he looked so worried about her. "I don't want to make you sad."

"What time are you leaving in the morning?" she whispered.

"I need to get up at oh-three-hundred, so I won't see you before I go. Don't cry," he said again, as a single tear rolled down her cheek.

"I know, I'm being silly. You've left a million times before, right?"

He thumbed away her tear as he shifted, his biceps bunching. She felt safe and content here beneath him, with the weight of Tyler's large body holding her down. She never really considered herself the type of woman who'd surrender to a man, but she loved feeling his powerful body above hers. She was at his complete and utter mercy and loved it.

Tyler kissed her lightly once more and then rolled them, so she was nestled between the back of the sofa and him. "I have left before," he said in a low voice, "but we weren't together then. I never had qualms about leaving, either. It feels different this time because it is."

"This is so fast though," she said worriedly. "How can I be this upset that you're going?"

"It is, and it isn't. I've known you for nearly a year, Rach. Maybe we didn't get together until now, but we know more about each other than most other new couples. I've seen you almost every day, unless I'm deployed. In some ways I know you better than women I've dated for months. And like I said before—I noticed you. I wasn't going to make a move since I thought you weren't available, but hell, sweetheart. You're impossible not to notice."

Her mouth parted, but no words came out.

"I love holding you close like this," he said quietly. His hand ran over her hair, and she couldn't believe this big, macho guy could be so tender.

"I want you to stay here tonight—not have sex," she hastily added. "I just want you to hold me before you have to go. I know you need to sleep, but I don't want to be alone. You're right next door and—"

"I'll stay with you, Rach," he said, interrupting her. He kissed her gently. "But only if you're sure you're okay with that. I'd never presume anything. I love the idea of sleeping with you in my arms, but I can wait."

"I know. I trust you, Tyler. I want you to stay here."

"I already finished packing up my clothes and gear. I need to set the alarm on my phone for quite early though."

"That's fine. And you'll sleep okay, here? I just realized you might be too tired for your mission if you don't get a good night's sleep. Maybe this was a bad idea."

"Sleeping with you in my arms won't be a hardship, Rach," he assured her. "We're used to sleeping anywhere. Trust me when I say a soft bed with you in my arms sounds like heaven."

"Okay," she said, suddenly feeling shy.

"Is it okay if we go to bed early though? Normally I'm an early riser, but three a.m. is pushing it. I'll go grab my phone charger so I can plug it in here. We don't usually bring phones on missions, but I'll leave it with my stuff on base. I want it fully charged for when I get back."

"Oh, yeah, that's fine."

"Okay. I'm going to run next door, grab it, and double-check that everything's in order for tomorrow. Lock the door behind me, okay? I'll knock quietly in a few minutes."

Tyler stood and then helped her up. He undid the lock, frowning slightly. "When I get back, I'll help you put a stronger lock on here."

"I can probably do it or hire a handyman or something."

"There's no need, since you have me to help you," he said, ducking down for another quick kiss. She stared up at him, feeling slightly off-kilter. "I'll be quick. See you in a few minutes. Don't forget to lock the door behind me."

A beat later, he was striding toward his own

apartment. Her heart clenched. She'd miss him so much when he was gone, and it was silly to get so attached to Tyler so quickly. She wouldn't normally invite a man into her bed so fast, but she felt safe with him. And what if something happened to Tyler while he was gone? She didn't want to miss the chance to sleep in his arms, to feel his strength and heat and breathe in his scent. She had no idea how long he'd be gone. She just knew she'd miss him like crazy.

# Chapter 8

Tyler's phone vibrated at oh-three-hundred, waking him from a deep sleep. He jerked awake, blinking as he remembered he was still in Rachel's bed, and quickly fumbled for his phone on the nightstand. Tyler swiped the screen to shut off the alarm, but Rachel was already stirring beside him. He set his phone down and curled back around her, knowing he had to get up in mere moments.

She sighed contentedly in her sleep, and he nuzzled closer, loving the feel of her soft curves pressed up against him.

He'd come back to Rachel's apartment last night to find her in sleep shorts, a strappy camisole, and long cardigan. She'd looked slightly nervous, and he'd quickly tugged her into his arms for a hug, asking if she'd be more comfortable if he left and slept at his own place. Biting her lip, she'd shaken her head and then guided him down the hallway to her bedroom.

There'd been nothing sexier than her hand in his as she led him further into her apartment. Even knowing he wasn't going to strip her bare and kiss her soft skin everywhere, he'd been hard. Rachel was irresistible. She was beautiful and sweet. Although he knew holding her close all night long would make it that much harder to leave early this morning, he couldn't have turned down her invitation if he'd wanted.

They'd passed her daughter's bedroom on the way, with Rachel taking one last peek inside to make sure she was down for the night. It was humbling to know Rachel trusted him enough to stay here with both her and her daughter. Aside from her ex-boyfriend, he'd never even seen another man here since they'd moved in. Tyler knew she wouldn't let just anyone into her life, and although they were still new as a couple, he loved that she wanted him here.

Tyler would do everything he could to show Rachel he was serious about her. That he could be the man she needed in her life. It was hard to believe he had such strong feelings for her so soon, but she was everything he'd wanted in a woman—smart, caring, independent, with just a hint of shyness that made his own protective instincts rise. She might not need a man to provide for her, but hell if Tyler wouldn't love taking care of both her and her daughter. Just being near Rachel made him smile, and that told him everything.

Whereas in past relationships, something never felt quite right, things just clicked between them. He realized it was only the beginning, but hell. It felt so natural holding her in his arms, he didn't want to get up and leave her.

Rachel mumbled in her sleep, and Tyler pressed

his lips to her temple. He'd slept in boxers and a tee shirt, with Rachel's lithe body tucked against his. She was slender but had curves in all the right places. He'd been hard as she'd snuggled back against him, her ass nestling against his stiffening cock. He hadn't attempted to take things further than simply holding her, but his erection had been unavoidable. Rachel was tempting as hell. He knew she'd been aroused as well earlier when he'd kissed her on the sofa, pinning her beneath him, but he also respected her too much to push for anything more. They both needed to be ready.

"Tyler?" she mumbled as she stirred. "Is it already three a.m.?"

"Yeah, baby," he said softly, pressing his lips against her hair. "It's oh-three-hundred. I've got to go."

She shifted in his arms so that she was facing him, and even in the dim light coming from the hallway, he could see the swells of her breasts pressing against her camisole. Someday, he longed to tug her top down and kiss those perfect mounds, palming her breasts in his hands and sucking on those pert nipples. Tyler wanted to kiss her everywhere, to drive her out of her mind with pleasure.

What would it feel like to sink between her thighs, thrusting his aching cock into her velvety walls and rubbing her clit until she came?

He stiffened uncomfortably, knowing he had to be good. His body had a mind of its own though, and he reached down, shifting his aching erection. "Sorry," he murmured, hoping that didn't make her uncomfortable.

Rachel's cheeks were flushed, and even in her half-sleepy state, he could tell she was as affected as him. Her eyes were wide with arousal, her quickened breathing causing her breasts to rise and fall. He reached over to brush some of her hair back, then shifted, rolling them over so he was straddling her. Her arms and legs immediately wrapped around him, as she gasped as his erection nudged at her core.

He kissed her lightly, loving the way she whimpered and clung to him as his arms caged her in. He slid his fingers into her hair, his thumb lightly caressing her temple. "I'll miss you, Rach."

"I'll miss you more. I wish you didn't have to go."

"I know, baby," he said, kissing her again. Rachel was soft and pliant beneath him, and he'd love more than anything to spend the rest of the morning thoroughly exploring her body. Even if they didn't have sex yet, he could touch her. Taste her.

Except he had to leave.

He deepened the kiss, letting his tongue slide into her mouth, and Rachel eagerly kissed him back, finally bucking up against him once. He groaned. "You feel so good, sweetheart," he murmured, reluctantly pulling back to gaze down at her.

"So do you," she gasped. "You're big and thick."

"Damn," he muttered, ducking for one more passionate kiss before he reluctantly pulled away and stood. "I'm going to need a cold shower before I head in to base." She giggled, and his lips quirked. "We'll have plenty of time to be together when I get back," he said, not sure if he was trying to reassure himself or Rachel. "I'm beginning to see that living next door will have some advantages."

Rachel climbed out of bed, turning on the lamp on her nightstand. He could see her face was flushed, her lips swollen from his kisses. Her breasts pressed against her thin camisole, looking so damn tempting. Tyler wished like hell he could ease her back into bed and kiss her everywhere, making her fall apart in his arms. He wasn't going to touch her intimately for the first time and then rush out the door. Rachel deserved to be savored. Cherished. He wanted to take his time, exploring her slender body and sexy curves.

His own cock was stiff and aching, but he'd just have to deal with it.

"I guess it does," she said, sounding slightly breathless. "I haven't dated at all since having Keira, but having you next door will make things easier. Not that dating with a five-year-old ever could truly be easy."

"You can stay in bed," he said, ducking down to tug on his jeans. He carefully zipped them up over the ridge of his erection. Damn. He'd gone from asleep to alert and ready to go in minutes. Now he'd be thinking of that intense kiss and Rachel whimpering beneath him every time he was in bed. And they hadn't even gotten to the best part yet.

"No, it's fine. I'll walk you to the door."

She padded across her bedroom, not bothering to throw on her cardigan this time. Rachel in her camisole and sleep shorts was sexy as hell. As was standing beside the rumpled sheets of her bed. Tyler loved that she'd wanted him here in her bedroom—in her bed. Her hips lightly swayed as she moved, her fresh scent filling her bedroom. And that long, blonde hair trailing down her back? Hell. It physically hurt to have to leave her.

Tyler quickly finished dressing. He unplugged his charger, grabbing it along with his phone and keys, then crossed to the bedroom doorway. They were quiet as they walked down the hallway, not wanting to wake her daughter. Before Rachel could open the front door, Tyler lightly gripped her hip, backing her up against the door and kissing her once more.

Rachel's fingers splayed against his chest, and his cock twitched. He kissed her again, deeper, before finally easing back. Tyler rested his forehead against hers, both of them breathing hard. He had to go. Tyler didn't have a choice in the matter.

"Be careful when you're gone," she whispered. "I know you guys train a lot, but I'll still worry about you."

"I will be. And I'll text you the names of my buddies. If Kyle starts causing any trouble, call them. They're good guys and will help you out."

"Okay," she said, growing serious. "Be safe, Tyler."

"I will, baby. I'll call or text when I get back. I don't know how long we'll be gone, but reach out to my friends on the other team if you need something." He kissed her again, lightly, but then backed away so she could open the door. It was hard as hell to walk out of her apartment. He glanced back at her one last time, and then was stepping out into the still night, striding toward his own place. He needed to shower, dress, grab his packed bag, and roll into base. For a guy that had been in the military his entire adult life, who was used to picking up and leaving whenever duty called, this felt infinitely harder than anything he'd done in the past.

# Chapter 9

Two weeks later, Rachel glanced around her quiet apartment. Kyle was dropping off Keira in a couple of hours, and she couldn't wait for her daughter to come home. The judge had revised the visitation schedule, temporarily allowing Kyle two Saturdays a month. They'd agreed to wait until school was out to start overnight visits, but as of this summer, she'd have to let Keira go spend the night at his house every other week.

Rachel's stomach twisted. She'd never even spent a single night away from her daughter. It would kill her to have to let her go to her dad's. While divorced parents dealt with that all the time, she wasn't divorced. He'd never been there for bedtime stories or scary dreams or tears in the middle of the night. Kyle had gotten her pregnant and then abandoned her.

How could a judge just grant someone like that time with a child?

In hindsight, she wished she'd never taken child support from Kyle. If she'd gotten him to relinquish his parental rights, she wouldn't be in this situation. Money would've been tight perhaps, but she wouldn't be dealing with sending her daughter off with a man who was essentially a stranger. He wasn't exactly a deadbeat dad, given that he paid her on time every month, but geez. He certainly wasn't an exemplary parent either.

Her phone buzzed with a text, and she jumped, startled out of her thoughts.

*Keira is crying again. Can't you tell her to behave when she's with me?*

Muttering under her breath, she texted Kyle back. Keira rarely cried at all with Rachel unless she was hurt. She was a happy child. While she'd seemed to adjust to spending one day a month with Kyle, now that their visits were growing more frequent, she'd been getting upset. Just this morning she'd asked if Tyler was back yet because she'd rather play with him. It broke Rachel's heart. She quickly thumbed a response to Kyle.

*She's five. She doesn't cry when she's at home. What happened?*

It wasn't the first time he'd texted her today. She'd been mad they took her out to breakfast earlier because Rachel had already fed her, and she wasn't hungry. Then she'd been upset they wouldn't play soccer with her like Rachel and Tyler did. Lunch had involved some drama as well because she hadn't liked whatever Carly had made.

Rachel's phone began to vibrate again, and she swiped the screen to answer Kyle's call.

"What's wrong?" she asked.

"Keira's crying and wants to come home. Carly is upset now, too. Can't Keira play by herself for a little while? Does she expect you to entertain her all day when she's at your apartment?"

"Of course, she needs attention, Kyle," Rachel said. "She's a little kid."

"I had that entire swing set installed in my backyard for her to play on, and she got bored of it after a few minutes. We've got a playroom full of toys."

"She wants you to play with her. Talk to her. What were you doing?"

"Just trying to relax with a glass of wine. I had a late gig last night and didn't get to spend much time with Carly. We were trying to enjoy this bottle of Cabernet I picked up when I was in Napa. When Keira ran over to show me something, she almost knocked over the entire bottle. It wasn't cheap, Rachel. She needs to be more careful."

"Why were you drinking with her there anyway?" she asked, growing irritated. "She's only there for the day. You can relax this evening after you drop her off."

"Carly doesn't live here. She deserves some quality time with me on the weekends. We both work hard during the week."

"Good grief, Kyle. You're the one who pressed for more visitation with Keira."

"Carly wanted to spend time with my daughter. She loves kids. I didn't realize that Keira would require constant attention and cry so much. She's not an infant."

"Why don't you just bring her home early then? If this isn't working, I'm not sure how you expect overnights to turn out this summer."

A beat passed, and she could tell he was annoyed. "Yeah. Fine. I'll bring her back early today. I want you to talk to her about crying so much when she's here. It bothers Carly. And I'm not changing my mind about the summer. Carly wants her to stay some weekends with us."

Rachel clenched her jaw, growing more irritated by the moment. "Why don't you bring Carly when you drop off Keira?" she asked tightly. "I'd like to meet her since she's spending so much time with my daughter. Maybe I can give her some suggestions for caring for a five-year-old."

Kyle barked out a laugh. "Yeah. Let's do it. Be nice to her though. She's young."

"You're bringing her over now."

"Absolutely. We'll be spending more time with Keira, like you said, so I'd like you both to meet. I'm glad I thought of it. See you soon."

Rachel opened her mouth, but he'd already ended the call. Shaking with anger, she set her phone down. She was positively fuming. Kyle couldn't be a bigger ass if he tried, and she was trying to remember what she'd found so attractive about him in the first place. Jesus. She'd actually slept with this asshole. Here she and Tyler hadn't done more than kiss and make out, and she'd actually had sex with this creep.

Rachel was on birth control and didn't plan to get pregnant unless she got married someday, but she had a feeling if things progressed with Tyler and somehow she did accidentally end up pregnant, he'd be nothing like Kyle. He certainly wouldn't disappear for years and then show up wanting to see his kid to impress a woman. Good grief.

Although she tried to remain positive about Kyle for her daughter's benefit, she just wasn't sure she could keep it up. Keira had heard them bickering in the past and no doubt would even more now. She hurried down the hall to her bedroom, running a brush through her hair and pulling it back into a ponytail. She put on her sneakers and grabbed her keys. She wasn't going to invite Kyle or Carly inside her apartment, but she could meet them down in the parking lot to chat.

Ten minutes later, she was sitting on the bench when Kyle pulled up in his BMW. She watched him get out of the car, frowning as he rounded the front and opened the door for Carly before helping Keira out. Carly was a grown woman. You'd think Kyle would help a young child before a fully capable adult. A busty blonde stepped out of the vehicle, clinging to Kyle's hand. She wore heavy makeup, and her hair looked like it had been bleached platinum. This woman had on a short dress and stiletto heels—not exactly what most women would wear on a Saturday afternoon at home. She clutched her designer handbag as Kyle shut the door, and then he finally was opening Keira's door. Rachel stood up from the bench, waving, as Keira climbed out of the car and began racing toward her. She cringed as she realized Kyle and Carly were so wrapped up in each other, they didn't seem concerned that a five-year-old was alone in the parking lot.

"Look out for cars!" she shouted.

Keira slowed and dutifully looked left and right before running straight into her arms. Kyle and Carly were slowly walking toward them, hand-in-hand. They couldn't go quickly given the ridiculous shoes she had on. Who wore those to watch a Kindergartner?

"I just had to wear my new Louboutin's," Carly gushed as she saw Rachel looking at the stilettos. "Kyle bought them for me. Isn't he sweet? I can't wait to wear them later on—with nothing else," she added with a giggle as she batted her eyelashes at Kyle.

Kyle smirked as he realized Rachel had overheard that part of the conversation. "She does love her designer bags and shoes, and I love to spoil her." His gaze flicked toward the apartment building and then around the parking lot. Although some people did drive expensive vehicles, his shiny BMW with custom rims stood out amongst the other cars. He'd done well for himself over the years. Either that, or he was drowning in debt. He paid child support every month but clearly had extra money to spend. "You really should think about getting a house, Rachel. Keira loves having my yard to run around in."

"I do not! You wouldn't even play soccer with me or push me on the swings. Mommy, is Mr. Tyler home yet?" Keira asked, jumping up and down. "I bet he'd want to play soccer."

"Who's Tyler?" Carly asked, looking between them as Kyle glowered. "I'm Carly, by the way," she said, holding out a perfectly manicured hand. "Kyle said he thought it would be good for us to meet. I guess we never were properly introduced," she added with a giggle.

"Rachel," she said smoothly, shaking the younger woman's hand. "Tyler is my neighbor."

"He's great at soccer, but he's in the military, so he has to leave a lot," Keira said.

"Tyler, right. I saw him when I was here a few weeks ago," Kyle said. "At first I thought he was with the pizza delivery guy."

Rachel resisted the urge to roll her eyes. Like pizza delivery guys worked in pairs and carried the food right into the house. Kyle had seen both the pizza delivery driver and her Navy SEAL neighbor. He'd been intimidated by Tyler. Whereas Kyle had the skinny, rocker look going for him, Tyler looked like the athlete he was. He was tall and muscled, and she had no doubt Kyle would never be a match for a man like him.

Tyler didn't flaunt his strength, but the way he carried himself let everyone around him know he could handle the situation. She liked that about him. He always seemed comfortable with himself, yet in control, aware of his surroundings. His take-charge attitude made her feel safe.

"No, he definitely doesn't deliver pizzas," Rachel said. "Anyway, thanks for bringing Keira back early. We'll talk later," she added, eyeing Kyle.

"I'm not changing my mind about this summer," he said in a low voice. "I agree waiting for school to end makes the most sense before disrupting her schedule, but I deserve more time with my daughter. We deserve more time," he added, his gaze shifting to Carly.

"I've always wanted kids," Carly gushed. "Keira is so adorable and looked so cute playing in our backyard. We'll probably end up getting a nanny or something to help out the weekends Keira is with us. We don't live together yet," she added with a giggle, "but someday soon that'll change."

"We're going ring shopping today," Kyle confirmed.

"I'm so excited, Kyle. I know just the type of ring I want, but I'll let you surprise me. I can't wait to try some on though. Did you know that one place serves champagne while you shop? It'll be fabulous."

Kyle looked over to say goodbye to Keira but was interrupted.

"Bye, Keira, baby!" Carly gushed. "We'll miss you! Next time you come over we'll do manicures together like I promised. Don't you want pretty pink nail polish like mine?"

She waggled her fingers, and Keira pressed closer to Rachel, eyeing the blonde suspiciously. Rachel's stomach churned. From what Kyle had said earlier, they'd barely played with her at all. What made Carly fawn over her daughter now? Frowning, she said goodbye to them both, taking her daughter's hand and hurrying toward her apartment.

"Mommy, I don't like her," Keira said.

Rachel glanced over at her daughter. "I know, sweetie. But Kyle is your dad, and that's his girlfriend. If they end up getting married someday, you'll see her a lot."

"Hmph. I don't want to see either of them. Just you and Mr. Tyler."

"Did you have any fun today?" she asked, trying to lighten the mood.

"No. They wouldn't play with me, and Carly showed me these dumb dresses she bought. I'm not wearing them, and she can't make me."

They walked up the stairs to her apartment, and Rachel glanced back toward the parking lot. She was surprised to see Carly watching them. The woman looked startled for a beat and then waved at them both. A moment later, she was sidling up to Kyle, sliding her manicured hand up his bicep. He backed her up against his BMW, kissing her deeply, and Rachel hastily looked away.

She needed to contact her lawyer. The law firm she worked at dealt with real estate. The attorneys weren't versed in domestic situations like child custody, visitation, etc. She'd have to contact her own lawyer and possibly find another one if she couldn't get the visitation schedule amended. The thought of sending Keira to Kyle's house for entire weekends starting this summer made her nauseous. Carly was young, but something just seemed a little off. She acted like she wanted to spend time with her but instead was relaxing with Kyle and talking about hiring a nanny. Not to mention the fact that there was something really fake about her—and not just her boobs. She tried to hide her laughter.

"What's so funny, Mommy?"

"Nothing," she said, smiling down at her daughter. "Did you eat dinner yet? Maybe we can go out to dinner tonight and celebrate that you're back home."

# Chapter 10

Tyler scrubbed a hand over the stubble on his face, frowning as he glanced over at his teammates. Their op hadn't gone as planned, with the team only rescuing three of the Americans from Pakistan. The former military DOD contractor and diabetic woman were still missing, having been taken to a separate location by the terrorists. The team had landed at Joint Base Andrews, outside of Washington, DC, so the three hostages they had rescued could be reunited with their families. After refueling, they'd hopped back on the plane for the cross-country flight, finally making it back to the West Coast.

It had been a grueling two weeks, trekking through the mountains of Pakistan when one lead after another had proved to be a dead end. Kalmati's men had been one step ahead of them, moving the remaining hostages before they could be rescued. The SEALs hated knowing they'd left the sick woman and military veteran behind. With additional intelligence, Tyler hoped they'd deploy again soon to finish the mission.

The men were somber as the plane banked to the left, beginning its gradual descent as they flew toward San Diego. Upon landing, they'd have to put away their gear, debrief with their commander, and be updated on any new information. Tyler was looking forward to a shower and shave as well. And he needed to text Rachel.

Sleeping on the hard ground for weeks hadn't been anything like sleeping with her in his arms, safe in her bed. Would she want him to spend the night again? The memory of kissing her against her apartment door right before he left was seared into his brain.

Relationships were tough for teams guys. Being in the Special Forces meant he deployed frequently, usually without much notice. Rachel needed a stable environment for her daughter, and Tyler worried she'd rethink things the longer he was gone. He couldn't wait to see her, touch her, and hold her close. Everything between them was new though. He had no right to sleep in her bed again, but hell if he didn't want to hold her close at night and feel her soft curves against him.

Brian shifted across the aisle of the C-17 cargo plane, restless, and Tyler's gaze flicked toward him. His friend was frowning, his fists clenched. "You okay, Blaze?" Tyler asked.

He shook his head, scrubbing a hand over his face. "I can't believe we left two hostages over there, man. And that woman with State? Hell. She could be in bad shape. Did I ever tell you my sister's diabetic?"

"Shit, no," Tyler said. "Is that why you look so concerned?"

"Yeah, partly. Obviously I don't like the idea of any woman being held against her will, but she's even more fragile than others because of her health. We don't know how much insulin she has with her. I've seen my sister struggle when her blood sugar gets too low. I know she's careful to travel with extra, but this woman was kidnapped. Even if she had additional insulin, they probably confiscated it. She could be in a damn coma by now, barely hanging on, and we're flying back home."

Tyler clenched his jaw. "If they want to keep her alive, they might allow her to use it. Why would they move her around to different locations if she was barely conscious? They could've taken another prisoner with them instead. You're right though. She probably didn't have a two-week supply of insulin on her and might not have much more time."

Brian muttered a curse, frowning. "I'm going to talk to the CO. It burns me up that we left when we were so damn close."

"None of us wanted to come home without completing the entire mission," Tyler countered. "We need solid intel though. Two weeks was a damn long time trekking through that rough terrain. They were dicking us around, making us think they were in one location and then vanishing."

"I wish we'd kept looking," Brian muttered. "Don't get me wrong. I'm happy as hell we rescued three Americans, but Jesus Christ. It blows that we left two behind, you know?" He huffed out a breath, shaking his head.

Tyler remembered looking at the pictures of the

missing Americans earlier that day. The woman had strawberry blonde hair and a light dusting of freckles across her cheeks. She was in her mid-twenties, and Tyler wondered what an innocent-looking woman like her did for the State Department. She could've been anything—a linguist, IT specialist, or even a foreign service officer. He hadn't read through her background in detail, although they had all the information on file. The team had been more concerned with the physical capabilities and health condition of the hostages. It didn't matter what she did when their mission was to rescue her. Tyler had been more concerned about the terrorists holding her against her will than her particular skillset.

Brian seemed to have taken a special interest in her. They didn't know the woman though, so he was no doubt just concerned for her safety. None of them wanted to think about what likely happened to a woman being held captive by terrorists. And he probably felt a connection to her because he was familiar with his sister's condition.

Ace came down the aisle of the cargo plane, sinking into a seat near them. "ETA is twenty minutes," he said. "The CO wants to have our AAR immediately, and I have a feeling that will be several hours given the fact that two hostages are still over there. Hell. I really want to get home to see Addison, but that will have to wait."

Havoc glanced over from where he was sitting nearby. "You'll get your pussy later, Ace. What about the rest of us? We need to head to a bar and meet some pretty women before we can get laid. Well, maybe not Trigger," he added with a smirk. "But we won't exactly be going out when we're spending hours doing the After-Action Report."

"Jesus," Ace muttered, glaring at him. "Don't talk about Addison like that."

"And leave Rachel out of it," Tyler warned, eyeing his teammate.

"Sorry," Havoc quipped, not looking sorry at all. "I'm just saying, you know you've got someone keeping your bed warm. What's a few more hours away from her? You'll see her tonight."

Tyler exchanged a glance with Ace, but Havoc was already putting on his headphones, ignoring the rest of them. Fifteen minutes later, the plane was making its final descent. They landed and disembarked, striding down the ramp. Tyler and his teammates headed toward their lockers, putting their weapons and equipment away. Tyler was itching to text Rachel, but he was nervous, too. He'd been out of contact with her for two entire weeks. What if she'd met someone else and decided dating a military guy was too much trouble?

Ace dropped some of his own gear down, his gaze shifting to Tyler. "Add just texted me. Apparently, she and Rachel got together once while we were gone."

"Oh yeah?" Tyler asked in surprise. The women had each other's numbers but barely knew one another. Their initial meeting at the barbeque hadn't lasted long. He hoped their meetup had gone well. It was rough on the family members left behind during missions. The team had only been gone for two weeks, but unlike a traditional military deployment, where families knew when to expect the return of their loved ones, Tyler and his teammates couldn't share anything like that. They couldn't call or email during their downtime. They didn't do video chats. They were literally trekking through dangerous enemy territory, pitching tents and sleeping on the hard ground. It was rough for everyone.

"Yep. I think Rachel's daughter was there, too. It sounded like Add appreciated having someone to talk to. I hate that we need to leave them behind. I know Raptor's team used to complain about leaving their girlfriends and wives, but hell. It's rougher than I expected."

"Isn't that the truth," Tyler said. "And Rachel isn't even my girlfriend."

"Oh no?" Ace asked, his lips quirking.

"Well, we haven't exactly discussed it," Tyler admitted. "I'm certain she's not seeing anyone else."

"Tell her you're not either," Ace suggested.

"Shit. You're right. She knows I'm into her and didn't like leaving her behind, but why beat around the bush? I might as well just tell her I want to be exclusive. I care about her."

"Yeah, do it, Trigger. I'm giving Addison a call before I hit the shower. See you at the AAR."

Anxiously, Tyler turned on his cell phone and quickly thumbed a text. He didn't have any messages from Rachel, but she'd known he was gone. There was no reason for her to text him while he was deployed.

*Hey Rach. Just got back, but I'll be on base several hours. Can't wait to see you.*

He hit the send button before he could change his mind. He'd missed her a crazy amount given they hadn't even been together long. He'd known guys in serious relationships who had things go sour while deployed. It sucked but wasn't uncommon. He hoped like hell she'd think he was worth it, that waiting around while he was on missions wasn't a dealbreaker. Tyler understood why most of his teammates were single though. It was tough to start anything up with their training and deployments.

He grinned when her reply lit up his screen.

*You're back? I missed you so much!*

*Can you come over later?*

His heart pounding in his chest, Tyler quickly swiped the screen to call her. Ace chuckled but was moving across the caged locker area to call Addison. "We're meeting with the CO at seventeen hundred," Ace said.

"Roger," Tyler said with a nod. Ace was smiling as he called his girl, and Tyler knew he was smiling like an idiot as well.

Rachel picked up on the second ring, sounding breathless with excitement as she answered.

"Hey baby," Tyler said. "We just got in."

"Oh, thank God. I was so worried about you. I didn't know how long you'd be gone, or when to expect you back, and I finally texted Addison one day. She's really nice, by the way. I'm just so glad you're home and safe. It sucked walking by your apartment door every day and knowing you weren't here."

Tyler's chest clenched. He hated that she'd been worried about him. He did have a dangerous career, but the team trained hard and was prepared for multiple situations. "I'm sorry you were worried, Rach. I thought about you and Keira a lot, too. How's she doing?"

"Okay, but Kyle is being a pain in my ass. He brought her home early again the other day. Anyway. I'll tell you about it later. Can you come over tonight?

I can't wait to see you, but I understand if you're exhausted and just want to crash."

"Yeah, I can come by, but I'm not sure how late I'll be. We have to debrief with our commander. We literally just flew in. I stashed my gear and then called you."

"I'm glad," she admitted, shyly. He could almost picture her flushing on the other end of the line.

"Me too. I love hearing your voice. You don't know how rough it was being away from you," he added quietly.

"I was worried you'd forget about us or something," Rachel said.

Tyler stilled. "Hell no. I thought about you all the time. Did you forget where I spent the night before I left? Or our kiss goodbye? You make me happy, Rach. Both you and Keira. We'll talk more later, but trust me when I say I missed you more than I want to admit.

"Okay," she said softly. "Are you heading to your meeting now?"

"Yep. Soon. I've got to shower and change, first," he added with a chuckle. "Let's just say we didn't exactly have luxury accommodations. I've got a short beard now, too. Keira probably wouldn't even recognize me. Don't worry, I'll shave before I come over."

"Okay, whatever you want. It doesn't matter to me. I just can't wait to see you."

"Me either. I'll text you when I'm heading out. It'll be a few hours though."

"I can wait. It's already been two weeks, so what's a little while longer. I'm so excited to see you."

"Me too, baby. I'll see you soon." Tyler was still

grinning as he ended the call. He had stuff here to deal with as they wrapped up everything from the mission, but he couldn't wait to get home. Normally, he'd be busy restocking his food, getting his laundry done, and doing all the other little things that required his attention. He lived alone and that had suited him fine. Tonight, he wanted to focus entirely on Rachel though. He couldn't wait to pull her close, kiss those soft lips, and tell her how much he'd missed her.

# Chapter 11

Tyler caught Rachel's hand in his, tugging her toward him as they strolled along the sunny beach the following afternoon. They'd grabbed a quick lunch at a café but were planning to enjoy a few hours of sunshine and sand together.

"I'm glad you could take the day off," Tyler said as he smiled down at her. "We usually get a few days of downtime after a deployment, but I realize you need to use your leave."

"Me too. I feel like I'm playing hooky or something going to the beach on a weekday, but honestly? I rarely take vacation days. I'll spend a week with Keira over the summer but otherwise tend to bank my leave. I never know if she'll be sick or something urgent will come up, so I like having all the time saved. They didn't mind since I never take personal days."

"That makes sense to save your leave, but you should take time for yourself every once in a while. You work hard, too."

"You're right. It's getting easier now that Keira's older. I swear little kids are constantly catching colds and getting sick. Oh, want to sit over there? It's not too crowded," she said, pointing to a spot twenty yards away.

"It works for me," Tyler agreed. Although Rachel had her straw beach bag slung over her shoulder, Tyler was hauling two chairs and a small cooler. His grip tightened on her hand, and she loved the connection between them. It had been so late by the time he'd gotten back to their apartment complex last night, they'd said hello and talked a little while, but then he'd crashed. She would've loved if he'd spent the night again, but she could tell how exhausted Tyler had been. Since she was getting up early to take Keira to school, he'd ended up going to his own place. Considering he hadn't been home in two weeks, she was sure he had plenty to do there. She'd missed him like crazy though.

She'd also felt almost shy about asking him to stay over again. Taking today to reconnect was absolutely perfect. Tyler's gaze was on her as she set her bag down in the soft sand and stood, smiling as she caught him watching her. "You look too tempting," he murmured, his lips quirking.

Her flowy coverup blew in the salty breeze, and she suddenly felt nervous. She was slender, but Tyler was in perfect physical condition. He had a tee shirt on over his board shorts, but it hugged his biceps and strong pecs. He lifted the chairs off his shoulder, easing them down to the sand as his muscles flexed.

Geez. He probably didn't have an ounce of fat on him. Rachel knew he had an extremely physical career and trained hard, but she felt nervous about letting him see her wearing so little.

She grabbed towels from her bag, draping them over the backs of the chairs to help weigh them down. Fortunately, there weren't any strong winds today. Tyler was setting the cooler down in the sand and kicking off his flip-flops. He tugged his tee shirt up and over his head, and she blinked, stunned. He wasn't self-conscious in the least and clearly had no reason to be. He was ripped, with six-pack abs and muscles toned from hours of training.

Quickly looking away, she slipped off her own sandals and pulled off her coverup. She'd chosen a more practical one-piece rather than a bikini. She tucked her coverup into her straw bag so it didn't blow away, grabbing her sunscreen.

"I love red on you," Tyler said, his eyes heating as his gaze briefly flicked over her. Her swimsuit had a high neckline, with a small cut-out, showing only a hint of cleavage. It was nice for running around with her daughter on the beach and not needing to worry about anything popping out. She wasn't into flashing her boobs to everyone in sight. This suit still flaunted her figure though, and she didn't miss the appreciation in his heated look.

She flushed but smiled up at him. "Thanks. You don't look so bad yourself," she teased. She lifted her sunglasses and winked as Tyler chuckled.

"Not so bad?" he asked with a laugh. "I'm just teasing you. You need help with your sunscreen?" he asked, nodding toward the bottle she'd grabbed.

"Um, sure, just on my back if you don't mind."

"My pleasure," he said quietly, taking it from her. Their fingers brushed against one another, and she swore sparks shot straight through her. She turned so her back was toward Tyler and pulled her blonde hair up into a mess bun, getting it out of the way. She felt him step closer, and it felt strangely intimate. He was taller than her and could look over her shoulder if he wanted, gazing down at her breasts.

Rachel felt oddly nervous, but then his big hands were spreading sunscreen over her shoulders and down her back, making sure to cover the cut-out area that exposed her skin. His touch was gentle and soft, and the scent of coconut filled the air. Tyler took his time, and she wanted to sigh in pleasure as she began to relax. His hands were muscular, but he was careful with her. And she probably loved his spreading sunscreen over her skin more than she should.

"I think we're good," he finally said, his voice thick.

"Thanks." She turned around and took the sunscreen bottle back, looking up at him. She couldn't see his blue eyes now that he'd put on sunglasses as well, but she still sensed the intensity of his gaze. Somehow having him gone for a couple weeks and then spending the day alone together made her feel like things had grown more serious between them. It was odd given the fact that she'd actually seen him less. Having him gone just made her realize how much she missed him. How much she'd already grown to care about him. Rachel knew he had a dangerous career. How many times had he left before?

Things were different now, and they both knew it. Without even realizing it, they had grown somewhat closer over the past few months, chatting a little more each time they saw one another around the apartment complex. Keira certainly loved to pepper him with questions. Rachel had been so focused on her daughter, she hadn't even considered a man like Tyler would be interested in her. She hadn't dated in years. But now that Tyler was right here in front of her? She knew she didn't want to let him go. She wanted to give them a chance, to see if their connection and chemistry could be something more.

"Want me to do your back?" she asked.

"Yeah, that'd be great. Thanks."

She tried not to stare as Tyler turned around, but goodness, he was gorgeous. She rubbed sunscreen over those broad shoulders and tanned, toned skin. Tyler stiffened slightly, and she knew he was affected by her touch. Rachel resisted the urge to step closer and kiss him between his shoulder blades. He was so close and oh so tempting. The muscles on his back rippled as he shifted in place. Tyler cleared his throat, and she realized she'd inadvertently stopped. She hurriedly finished up, enjoying the feel of his warm skin beneath her hands.

"How cold do you think the water is?" Tyler asked when she'd finished. "It's still early in the season. We wear wetsuits for training."

"I don't know—probably colder than I'd like. Let's go check it out though," she said, grabbing his hand and pulling him along with her toward the ocean.

He chuckled and let her guide him forward, then shocked the heck out of Rachel by scooping her up into his arms. She clung to him, laughing, and he jogged the rest of the way down to the water with her in his arms. She shrieked as she felt the cold spray of the Pacific. Although some people probably would still go in and freeze, she preferred the water at the end of summer when it was warmer.

"Don't drop me!"

He tightened his grip, holding her close. "I wouldn't drop you, Rach." She snaked her arms around his neck, looking up at him, and then Tyler ducked lower and kissed her softly. He tasted slightly of the beer he'd had with lunch and something else that was all musk and man. She shifted one hand to his cheek, feeling the slight stubble there. He'd shaved last night after getting home from his mission but already had a bit of scruff. It was sexy and arousing. She imagined his whiskers scraping over her sensitized skin as he kissed her everywhere.

Part of Rachel wished she didn't need to pick up Keira in a few hours. She'd love to have the evening alone with Tyler. Someday they'd have the quiet, romantic evening they wanted. Having the day together was perfect though, and her stomach fluttered with butterflies as he kissed her again.

Rachel whimpered softly as her hand moved to the nape of his neck, wishing they were alone somewhere, not on a busy beach. She knew Tyler would wait as long as she needed to progress their relationship further. No one would date a single mother and expect sex every moment. Normally, it was hard to find even a few minutes of free time. She was attracted to Tyler like crazy though, and his muscular arms holding her close made her nipples tighten and arousal pool at her core.

He lazily grinned down at her, and she knew her cheeks were flushed. Tyler could no doubt see the effect he was having on her. Her red swimsuit did nothing to conceal her taut nipples, and her breathing was coming in shallow gasps.

Tyler walked back to the sand and gently set her down, wrapping his arm around her waist. The cool water lapped at their legs, the breeze gently blew in off the ocean, and the sun shone brightly down on them. It couldn't have been a more perfect afternoon.

"I missed you so much, Rach."

"Me too. It was hard not seeing you every day. Keira really missed you, too."

He guided her back toward the chairs he'd set up in the sand, and they both sank down, stretching out their legs. Tyler reached over and grabbed some water bottles from the cooler, passing one to her after he'd opened it. "I'm sorry, baby."

She looked over at him in surprise. "You don't have to be sorry. That's your job, and I know you're good at what you do. I knew you were in the military long before you ever asked me out," she reminded him. "I knew how often you deployed."

"I know, but I also know it's hard being left behind, so to speak. It didn't matter as much when we were just neighbors. That reminds me, when I was running errands this morning, I picked up a new lock for you."

"You did?" she asked, looking over at him in surprise.

"Yep. I'll install it one night. I'd feel better when I'm gone knowing your place is more secure."

"Wow. Thanks. Just let me know how much I owe you for it."

Tyler waved a hand. "It's fine. You don't need to pay me anything. I want to do this for you."

"Tyler."

"You never said what happened with Kyle that had you upset," he said, changing the subject. She'd wondered if he'd done it on purpose so she wouldn't protest about the lock. Her mood had dampened at the mention of her ex, but she explained the custody situation to Tyler. She hadn't had time to update him last night, and she knew he was worried about it. "That's bullshit, Rach. He can't even handle a day with her. Why would he want an entire weekend?"

She blew out a sigh, glancing down at her red toenails. They happened to perfectly match her swimsuit. She felt pretty and sexy at the moment and didn't want to ruin her date with Tyler by talking about her problems. This was her life though, and she did appreciate his concern. "Yeah, it is bullshit. He's her father though, so unless he does something that's harmful or dangerous, there's not much I can do. Feeding her food she doesn't like isn't going to change anything. The courts would probably laugh me right out of there if I complained. Oh, and he hated when Keira said she'd rather see you than him."

Now it was Tyler's turn to look surprised. "She said that?"

"That she did," Rachel said with a smile, reaching over to take his hand. "She likes you. And she loves that you talk to her and actually pay attention."

"I like her, too. And her mother," he added with a wink. Tyler's thumb caressed the back of her hand, and she felt tingles spreading across her skin. She loved how attentive he was, but everything between them was still new. Exciting. What would it be like in six months? A year? She'd fallen fast for Kyle and ended up heartbroken. She and Tyler had great chemistry, but no one could predict the future.

"What are you thinking so hard about?" he asked gently.

"This. Us."

Tyler wove his fingers between hers, clasping her hand more tightly. "Well, I never expressly said it, Rach, but I don't want to see anyone else. You're the only woman I'm interested in. Hell, like I said, I would've asked you out months ago if I'd realized you were single. You're the only woman I want to kiss and have the right to spend the night with. Maybe things started out a little different because we're neighbors and already knew one another, but hell. I'd be crazy to let you slip through my fingers."

"So, you want me to be your girlfriend?" she teased.

"Hell yeah," he said immediately. "I want to be able to come over and see you and Keira after a long day, and to call you as soon as I get back from a mission. I know it can be rough dating a Navy SEAL given my dangerous job, but I promise I'll put you and Keira first. There will be times when I have to leave of course, but I'll do what I can to make life easier for you at home when I can't be here. I want to give us a real shot."

"So do I. When you were gone, it just made me realize all that much more how I'm already falling for you. I know it's fast and too soon to say it, but—"

"I'm falling for you too, Rach. Hell, I was already falling for you before I asked you out. My teammates all knew I was hung up on you. You make me happy," he admitted.

"You make me happy, too. And I love how sweet you always are."

"Just what every man wants to hear," he mock complained with a wink.

"And I like your muscles?" Tyler burst into laughter, and she squeezed his hand. "I mean, I do, but I like other things about you as well. I love talking to you and kissing you," she added, knowing that she was turning red.

"Me too, Rach. And seeing you in a swimsuit today has me wanting all sorts of things I shouldn't. I know you want to take things slow, and I can respect that, but hell. You're beautiful. Someday, when you're ready, I'm looking forward to seeing all of you. I've got no problem with waiting, but I am looking forward to the day I can make you mine completely."

"Will you stay over tonight? I know last night you were exhausted and needed to catch up on your sleep. I'm still not ready for us to have sex, but I loved having you hold me. And we'll just...take it slow. Let things happen naturally."

"Of course, I'll stay over. Anytime you want, as long as it won't be an issue with Keira. What time do you need to pick her up? We can grab some food for dinner and all eat together. Then play some soccer of course."

"Naturally," she said lightly, beaming at him.

"What?" he asked.

"I just love that you actually want to spend time with her. It sounds like Kyle and Carly want her to play alone at their house. His house. Oh, did I tell you they're planning to get engaged? And she wants to hire a nanny to watch Keira when she's over there every other weekend this summer."

"A nanny? Why? Do they work weekends?"

"Well, Kyle does have his music gigs, I suppose. I don't know what Carly does. It's like she wants the idea of having a child there but doesn't want to do any of the work. When they dropped her off the other day, I finally met her. She kept calling Keira 'baby.' It was kind of weird."

"Shit. I call you baby."

Her cheeks flushed. "Well, that's different. I think it's sweet when you say it, plus we're dating. She barely knows my daughter. I can't figure out what's off about the whole thing."

Tyler frowned. "Do you know her last name?"

"Well, no, I actually don't. Why?"

"I can have my buddy run a background check on her. Kyle, too. I know he's her father, but it might not be a bad idea, especially if she's going to start spending nights there sometimes."

"You'd do that for me?" Rachel asked, bewildered.

"Of course. I care about you, Rach. Keira too. Maybe Kyle made you think all guys are jackasses, but I'm not. Even if we eventually broke up for whatever reason, I'd still want you both to be safe."

Rachel's eyes watered as she looked over at him.

"What's wrong?" he asked, suddenly looking concerned.

"I just never really had anyone worry about me that way before. I guess my parents did when I was younger, but look how Kyle totally abandoned me. He didn't care that I was pregnant with his baby. He didn't have any interest in Keira until recently. I'm used to doing things on my own."

"I'm not him," Tyler said. "I understand why you're hesitant about some things—why you don't want to rush head-first into a relationship. I swear I'm not like that, Rach. It's okay if you don't fully believe that yet. I'll do whatever I can to show you I'm serious. I won't hurt you," he added softly.

Rachel blinked away her tears, suddenly feeling overwhelmed. "I do want to believe you, Tyler. I trust you, it's just—I'm scared."

"I know you are, baby. It's okay. We don't have to rush into things. And if you still want me to stay over tonight after we've spent the entire day together, there's nothing else I'd rather do."

"Do you have work tomorrow?"

"No. Our CO gave us several days off. I'll probably still be up fairly early to meet the guys for PT. We try to at least go for a run together even if we won't be training on base."

"Okay. I was worried you might want to sleep in. Keira's an early-riser."

Tyler's lips quirked. "I'm always up early, Rach. It's a habit from years of life in the military. Now, my wake-up call at oh-three-hundred the last time I stayed over was pushing it, even for me. But don't worry about Keira ever waking me up."

"Okay," she said, smiling at him and then glancing out at the waves crashing on the shore. It was a beautiful, sunny afternoon. She had an amazing man at her side. And at the moment, she felt happy. Safe. She pushed the tiny niggle of worry she still had about Kyle and Carly to the back of her mind. Keira wouldn't do any overnights until the summer, and in the meantime, she wanted to enjoy time with her daughter and new boyfriend.

# Chapter 12

"I ran those background checks," Ace said to Tyler a few days later, catching him in the locker room on base before they conducted drills on the water.

"Oh yeah? Did you find anything?" Tyler asked as he turned toward his team leader, immediately noticing the frown on Ace's face. The large man nodded, looking serious.

"I did, but not what I expected. Kyle has a clean record. Carly was arrested once years ago for breaking and entering."

"What?" Tyler asked, his mouth dropping open in surprise.

"Yeah. She was young—a teenager—and broke into the house of another family in the neighborhood. She stole some jewelry from the mom. The parents pressed charges, and the records were sealed because she was a minor. I noticed something off when I ran a background check, so I dug deeper.

"Shit. I don't want you getting into trouble, man. I appreciate you looking into their records though."

"No one will know I was in there," Ace assured him. "Her record seems clean after that incident, but I'm going to keep looking to see if I can find anything else. It was probably just a dumb teenage prank. She doesn't seem to be a hardened criminal or anything, but hell. You know as well as I do that even someone who seems innocent can do plenty of harm."

"Yeah, don't I know it. Rachel thought Carly had a strange interest in Keira. I don't know. I don't think anything specific happened, she just got a weird vibe from the woman. Plus, Rachel's ex never even had an interest in meeting Keira until he started dating this chick."

"That's messed up," Ace muttered. "How could he ignore his own child?"

"It's a damn good question. The hell if I know. The guy's a dick. Let me know if you find out anything else."

"Will do," Ace said.

"You think you and Addison will have kids some day?" Tyler asked. "You seem pretty happy together."

Ace chuckled. "Maybe someday, but not anytime soon. You guys left the barbeque early, but when Ghost's baby woke up, they were having a hell of a time. I felt bad for him and Hailey, but it also made me realize I'm not ready to be a father yet."

"Raptor said Hailey went back to work. She enjoys her job, from what I gather, but it sure would be tough working all day and then caring for an infant all night. And Ghost? Hell. He's still going on missions with Raptor's team. Rachel said she basically got no sleep when Keira was little. I don't know how they do it."

"You two seem serious already," Ace noted.

Tyler nodded. "We are. I used to see her all the time since we're neighbors. We'd talk, and Keira would ask me about a zillion questions and tell me every detail of her day, but I loved it. I'm kicking myself for not asking Rachel out sooner or realizing that Kyle was her ex."

Ace lifted a shoulder. "You thought she was with him. I don't blame you for not wanting to stir up problems. They have a child together."

"Yep. Anyway, I appreciate you running background checks on them. Let me know if you find out anything more about Carly. I don't know why Rachel got a weird vibe about her, but women seem to sense these things. My sister is always scarily accurate about predicting when something is up."

"Women's intuition, man," Ace said with a low laugh. "It's the real deal."

"What's up, fellas?" Mark asked with a grin as he sauntered into the locker room. He pulled open his locker, grabbing his wetsuit for their drill on the water. "Which women are we talking about here? Addison and Rachel?"

"Trigger's sister," Ace said.

Mark's head swiveled toward them. "Is she still planning to visit? If I remember correctly, you were going to rope her into babysitting."

Tyler shook his head. "She's not coming until next month. Her photo shoot thing got rescheduled. She's welcome to stay with me anytime, of course, but they're putting her up in a nice hotel, so she's going to combine business with pleasure."

"She's a model?" Ace asked.

"No. She's a blogger. Actually—Everly calls herself an influencer. My parents don't know what the hell that means, so I always say she blogs. Everly posts photos on social media and gets paid for it. Sometimes she partners with companies, but some places have affiliate links. She gets a small cut when people buy through her links. If you grow your following enough, suddenly you're making big bucks."

"So, she just posts photos of her life," Ace said, looking baffled.

"Yep. Some staged, some candid. She's always snapping pictures to use."

"I couldn't live like that," Mark said, shaking his head. "Documenting every piece of your life? Pulling your phone out to capture every single moment? No thanks."

"I don't think I'd like that either, no matter how much money I was making. When I'm online, I'll stick to gaming," Ace said. "That's mostly anonymous anyway, aside from my meeting Addison."

"I'd say that worked out pretty well for you," Mark said with a smirk.

They heard voices in the hallway, and then the rest of their teammates came walking in. All three of them were deep in discussion, and Brian looked unhappy. "What happened?" Ace asked.

"Blaze just talked to the CO," Rob said. "There's still no new intelligence on the two Americans being held in Pakistan."

"You know they won't send us in without pinpointing the exact location of the hostages," Ace said, his gaze landing on Brian.

"Understood," Brian said.

Tyler exchanged a glance with the other men. They all knew Brian had been particularly concerned. No one liked leaving Americans behind, especially a woman. Tyler just hoped she'd somehow gotten the insulin she needed. Otherwise, they'd only be rescuing one person when they returned.

"All right," Ace said, clapping his hands together as all eyes shifted to him. "We're heading out to the water in twenty. Change into your wetsuits and gear up. We've got multiple drills we'll be conducting, and it sounds like Raptor's team will be with us as well."

The men quickly began pulling things from their lockers and changing. Tyler's gaze shifted toward Brian. He still looked unhappy, but Tyler knew he'd be focused on the training. Leaving the woman behind in Pakistan had hit him harder than the others. Scrubbing a hand over his jaw, Tyler let his thoughts shift to the afternoon ahead and then unbuttoned his uniform. He couldn't worry about Brian or even the hostages right now. The team had work to do, requiring their full attention.

# Chapter 13

"Oh my God, this is so good," Rachel said, stretching her legs out on the grass in the common area of their apartment complex the following weekend. She smiled, looking at the sunlight beaming down on them, and then took another bite of her hamburger, the juicy tomato and tangy pickle combining perfectly with the charcoal-grilled burger.

"Hotdogs are better, Mommy," Keira said.

Tyler's lips quirked, and he flipped another burger on the community grill. "I have to admit, I never grilled out here before. I help Ace sometimes when he hosts, and we've had bonfires on the beach as well, but it's about time we tested out our apartment complex amenities."

"What's a bonfire?" Keira asked.

Rachel explained the concept to her daughter, her eyes flickering over to Tyler as he watched them. He'd slept in her bed every night since their date on the beach a week ago. It felt like everything had changed since the two-week mission his team had gone on. Somehow their relationship had fast-forwarded a bit when he'd gotten back. They still hadn't made love, but they'd kissed passionately every night, exploring one another's bodies more and more.

She felt a little guilty that she could never spend the night at his place, but they both realized it made more sense with Keira to stay at Rachel's. Tyler had put a new deadbolt on her front door, and she'd almost given him one of the keys. It seemed too soon for that, but goodness. She loved having him there every evening. He was nothing but patient and sweet with both her and Keira, and as for the way he made her heart race?

She wanted to shiver in delight.

Rachel felt so relaxed and happy in the sunshine, she wished every weekend could be like this. Of course, some days Tyler would have training or be deployed. Sometimes Keira would be at her dad's. But right at this exact moment?

Life was perfect.

"You look happy," Tyler commented, his eyes twinkling as he looked at her.

"I am happy," she confirmed, with a smile just for him.

He took the last of the burgers off the grill, stacking them on a platter and coming to sit beside them. She smiled as she watched Tyler stretch out on the pink picnic blanket. "I think I need one of these," he joked.

"I picked it out!" Keira said excitedly. "Pink is my favorite color. Well, maybe purple. No, pink."

"I love it," Tyler said, reaching out to lightly ruffle

her hair. She beamed up at him, and Rachel felt her heart clench. Tyler was great with her, and she wondered, not for the first time, if something long-term really would come of this. The possibility seemed almost too good to be true. She'd been on her own with Keira for so long, but Tyler seemed to genuinely care about them both. Could it really be that easy? The pieces of her life felt like they had finally fallen into place.

Keira took another bite of her hot dog, then brushed some hair back from her face. "Sweetie, you just got mustard in your hair," Rachel said with a laugh. She reached over with a napkin, trying to wipe it off.

"Good thing your hair is yellow," Tyler joked. "It matches the mustard."

"My hair isn't yellow. It's blonde!" Keira said, giggling hysterically.

"Oh, right. My bad," Tyler said, winking at her. He set his plate on his lap, taking a bite of his hamburger. "This turned out pretty good. We'll have to grill out here again soon."

They all finished eating, enjoying the beautiful weather. After dinner, they decided to take a walk rather than their usual evening activity of kicking around a soccer ball. Rachel was surprised her daughter had agreed to a walk, but Tyler turned it into a fun game by playing I-Spy with her along the way. He took Rachel's hand in his, his warm, calloused fingers sending shivers racing down her spine. Every time he touched her, she positively lit up. Rachel couldn't even explain what it was. Something about Tyler just drew her right to him.

Things had moved relatively fast between them. It

was only a month ago that they'd first begun dating. She'd known him for much longer than that and felt safe whenever he was near. Tyler was always doing little things to put her first, and she tried to reciprocate as much as she could. It was hard, when her young daughter had to be her priority right now.

Tyler gently eased her closer as they walked along, and when they saw a neighbor walking her dog as they came back to their apartment complex, Keira begged to go over and see them. Rachel gave her permission, and then she and Tyler were alone for a moment as her daughter ran ahead to the common area.

"This was fun, having our own little barbeque outside," Rachel said.

He gazed down, those light blue eyes searching hers. "It was. I'm looking forward to being alone with you later on, too," he said huskily.

Rachel felt a flush creep across her cheeks. Things had gotten further than ever between them last night, with Tyler kissing his way down her neck and across her cleavage while she lay gasping beneath him. She'd still left her camisole and sleep shorts on, but wow. She'd very nearly come apart in his arms just from his hands moving over her clothing. Butterflies filled her tummy. Tyler was so patient, but she wanted him. Needed him. She wanted Tyler to make love to her— to touch her everywhere. She needed him to pin her beneath him and slide inside her body, filling her in a way only he was capable of.

She'd been in lust before, but she'd never felt the way she did right now. Her body actually ached for him, and she couldn't stand the idea of waiting any longer for them to make love. She pressed closer to his muscular frame, rising up to lightly kiss his cheek and then whisper in his ear. "I don't want to wait anymore, Tyler."

His heated gaze locked on her, and he lifted his hand to the nape of her neck. His thumb trailed lightly over her skin, and the intensity in his eyes should've scared her. "Are you sure, Rach? I don't want to do anything you're not ready for."

She nodded. "I trust you," she said quietly. "And I want you. Every night you're so careful with me, but I'm ready for more. I need all of you."

His eyes glittered with lust, and he ducked down for a quick, chaste kiss. "How soon can we get Keira to bed?" he joked.

"Not soon enough," she admitted. "But maybe the walk tired her out." They both looked over to where she was running around with her neighbor's dog, happily laughing.

"She likes animals," Tyler commented. They stood there side-by-side, watching her, and he laced her fingers through his.

"She does. I wouldn't mind getting a dog but not while we're in an apartment. Maybe someday."

"Maybe someday," Tyler echoed. "I can picture a house, a yard with a dog and Keira running around in it." She looked up at him, and something passed between them. An understanding. Could she have a future like that with Tyler? It was too soon to be talking about white picket fences, but she absolutely could see herself with this man. Having a family with him. A future.

He lifted their connected hands to his mouth, brushing his lips softly over hers. Her heart fluttered. "Maybe we should get her inside and settled down,"

Rachel said. It felt weird planning that this would be the night they made love, but sometimes that's how life went when you were a parent. Every detail of her life had to be arranged, planned in advance. Tyler didn't seem to mind. He couldn't stop lightly caressing her, touching her, and pulling her close. She couldn't wait to have him all to herself later.

# Chapter 14

Rachel's stomach fluttered as she came into the bedroom that night, her heartbeat speeding up. She always checked on Keira before she went to bed, and although Rachel usually left her bedroom door cracked, tonight she softly closed it behind her. The door clicked shut, the silence of her bedroom surrounding them. Her hands were clammy, and she felt silly for being so nervous. It had literally been years since she'd been with a man though. She wasn't twenty-three anymore. Not that she was old at twenty-eight, but she'd had a baby. Her body wasn't exactly the same as it had once been.

Tyler smiled as she slipped off the satin robe she'd worn over her silky negligee, crossing the bedroom toward him. "I imagined you in something like that," he said huskily, moving closer and lightly running his fingertips up her bare arm. She could feel the heat of him in front of her, his fresh, earthy scent filling her bedroom.

"You did?"

"Why do you look so surprised?" His voice was lower than usual, and she could tell he was restraining himself. Holding back to make sure she was comfortable. "You're beautiful," he murmured huskily, taking the silky robe from her hand and tossing it onto the bed. "And the first time we went out—to the barbeque at Ace's—you had on that sexy, floral blouse. For some reason it reminded me of lingerie. But this? Wow. I mean you'd look gorgeous in anything, Rach, but I almost have no words for how incredible you look."

She glanced down, flushing, and felt her nipples pebbling beneath the silk. The top of the chemise was trimmed in lace, with thin straps holding it up. The short negligee hit the top of her thighs, barely covering her ass. She'd put on the matching thong beneath it, with a tiny scrap of fabric that covered her mound. She felt oddly nervous, despite the fact that Tyler's hands had moved over her body each night. He'd never seen her naked, and the lingerie she'd chosen for tonight was revealing. Provocative.

Tyler's eyes were heated as he gazed at her, and he ducked down for a kiss, his large hands cupping her face. Her pulse pounded, and then she was whimpering as his lips moved to her neck, his hands skimming down her body and gripping her hips. "You're so sexy and gorgeous," he said, his voice thick. He nipped at her tender flesh, his teeth grazing her neck.

She clutched onto him, pressing closer, and felt his erection through his boxers. Tyler was thick and hard. She couldn't wait to feel him inside her. It felt like every nerve-ending in her body was sensitized, on high alert. The second Tyler entered her, she'd explode. She'd been thinking about this moment for weeks—of Tyler's large body pinning her down, his thick cock penetrating her. Some women might have trouble reaching orgasm, but she was lucky. Sex when she was younger had always been pleasurable and fun. She was still nervous given that it had been a long time, but she knew he'd never hurt her.

He kissed her neck again, softly sucking on her skin. One hand moved to her ass, and he groaned as he realized she had on a thong. He moved over her bare cheeks, seemingly unable to stop touching her. Arousal dampened her folds, and she whimpered in surprise as he suddenly bent and lifted her into his arms. Tyler held her like she weighed nothing at all, turning and then laying her on the bed. He gazed down at her a beat, taking in the way her breasts moved up and down, pressing against the silk. Her mouth parted, and she watched as Tyler stripped his shirt off, tossing it to the floor. He was muscular and mouth-watering. She'd seen him shirtless before but wow.

His cock tented his boxers, but he didn't remove them yet. "Tyler," she whispered. He paused for just a moment longer and then was ducking down to kiss her. Devour her. Tyler moved over her body, and his large hands cupped her breasts, kneading them. She whimpered as he kissed his way across her collarbone, moving lower. He kissed one breast through the satin and lace, his hand sliding up her inner thigh to cup her mound. She was already wet, dripping for him, and she flushed as she realized he'd know how aroused she was. Tyler growled in approval, touching her intimately through the scrap of fabric. He found her clit, rubbing in a small circle, as she gasped and bucked up towards him.

"Let's get this off you," he murmured, his hands gripping the bottom of her chemise. He eased it slowly up her body, and she trembled beneath him, her breathing coming in shallow gasps. The air washed over her bare breasts, and she resisted the urge to cover herself. Rachel had nothing on but her skimpy thong, lying there in the sheets. Tyler stilled, staring down at her. Her blonde hair fanned out, spilling around her breasts, and he looked at her like a man starved. "You're so beautiful, baby. So damn gorgeous." One hand skimmed over her breast, his calloused fingers gentle on her tender skin. His thumb grazed her nipple, and he looked at her almost reverently.

He ducked and kissed one breast, his mouth hot as he moved over her. She gasped at the intimacy of the moment, practically shivering in delight as his breath fanned over her skin. He kissed her breast again, more firmly, and then his wet tongue was laving against her nipple as she moaned in pleasure. Tyler took his time, enjoying her, and she clutched onto his muscular shoulders, lost in the moment. He shifted slightly, and she felt his erection brushing against her thigh. Tyler was hard. Ready. He was focused only on her though.

Rachel had always been sensitive, but Tyler's mouth against her breast nearly had her coming undone. He sucked one nipple into his mouth as she gasped. Although her ex-lovers had certainly enjoyed her, she'd never been with a man as attentive as him. It was like every other man paled in comparison.

Tyler moved to her other breast, kissing around her areola and then suckling her. Her hands flew to his head, holding him against her as she squirmed. His hand slid to her sex, and he rubbed her clit through the silk as he tongued her nipple. "Tyler!" she cried out.

"Do you need to come, baby?" he asked, lightly biting her nipple before softly blowing on it. His thick fingers circled her clit, her silken arousal dampening her panties. She was drenched for him, and he didn't let up, just circled her tender bud until she couldn't hold back a moment longer. Tyler flicked his tongue over her nipple, never stopping his ministrations, and suddenly it was too much to bear, and she cried out quietly in her bedroom.

Waves of pleasure washed over her, and Tyler captured her cries with his mouth, letting her ride out her orgasm. He softly kissed his way down her body, nuzzling against the scrap of fabric covering her sex. "You smell so good, Rach."

She flushed with embarrassment, but Tyler's thick fingers were already sliding beneath the straps of her thong, tugging it off. He ran his hands up her thighs, parting them as he edged closer. "I'm going to taste you, Rach, and then you're going to come again for me." Before she could even utter a word, he was lifting her legs over his broad shoulders.

She was exposed. Bared to him. Her hands clung to his head, and then suddenly Tyler was tasting her, lapping at her arousal, his tongue trailing through her drenched folds. Tyler kissed her sex, having no qualms about tasting all of her. Rachel was still slightly embarrassed, but then his tongue trailed up her slit, finding her swollen bud, and she cried out.

He sucked her clit between his lips, and she was so sensitive from her first orgasm, she gasped as pleasure shot straight through her. Two thick fingers slid into her channel, and then Tyler simply devoured her, sucking on her clit and thrusting his fingers until she was raking her fingernails over his head and crying out his name in pure ecstasy.

\*\*\*

Tyler pulled Rachel more tightly against him, loving the feeling of her warm body naked and safe in his arms. They'd made love once earlier after he'd pleasured her, and it was everything he'd imagined. He could tell she'd been nervous when he'd gone down on her, but hell. Eating Rachel out had been amazing. She might've been hesitant at first, but then she'd been so excited, she'd raked her nails through his hair, her lower lips quivering against his mouth as he made her come. Hard.

Tyler had wanted to roar in approval at making his girl come twice so quickly. His hands and mouth on her had been pure heaven. Tyler had been hard as steel after that, but he'd made love to her slowly, wanting to remember each moment. He'd positioned Rachel beneath him, and they'd both gasped as he'd penetrated her, claiming her body as his own. Tyler had pinned her hands to the bed, lacing their fingers together, and she'd surrendered to him, sweetly crying out his name once more as he'd made her come.

And right now?

He couldn't stop touching her soft skin, running his hands over her curves, and kissing her everywhere. She mumbled in her sleep, pushing her ass back against his stiffening cock. He bucked against her lightly, then reached around to touch her pussy.

"Tyler," she whimpered.

He softly kissed her bare shoulder. "I want to take you again, Rach."

She started to shift in his arms, trying to turn onto her back, but he settled her. "No. Stay just like this, baby." He managed to grab a condom from the box on the nightstand, sliding it onto his erection. Tyler eased one of her legs up, then slid into Rachel from behind.

"Oh God," she moaned. "That feels so good. You're so big."

Her inner walls clamped down around him, still wet with her arousal. He reached around and rubbed her clit, enjoying her tiny gasps of pleasure as he slowly moved in and out. Tyler took his time, loving her moans and the feel of her pussy clamping around him. He could tell she was getting closer, and she cried out as he strummed faster against her swollen bundle of nerves.

"Come for me again, baby," he murmured, squeezing one breast as he increased the pace of his thrusts. She was so wet, his cock easily moved in and out of Rachel's body. He was big, but she was swollen and ready, easily taking him.

"Harder, Tyler," she whispered.

He tightened his arm around her and bucked harder, his balls tightening. Someday he'd love to bend her over in bed and take her from behind. He couldn't get as deep from this angle, but hell if he didn't love holding her in his arms while he claimed her. He could tell she was on the edge, and as he rubbed her clit again, she finally surrendered to him, crying out his name again and again.

Tyler stiffened behind her and thrust once more, his own orgasm more intense than ever before. This woman was it for him. Everything about her called out to him. She made him happy with her genuine smile, but it was more. He wanted to protect her and fight all her battles. Hold her when she was sad and share passionate moments like this, where their bodies were connected, and they were truly joined as one.

"My God," she whimpered as he carefully eased out of her. Tyler strode to the bathroom, disposing of the condom, then came back and pulled her into his arms. Rachel eagerly snuggled into him, her head on his shoulder, her arm wrapped around his waist, and her legs intertwined with his. She was sexy and beautiful, and he'd do everything in his power to keep her in his life. Tyler hadn't waited this long to find her to not give her everything.

# Chapter 15

The next month passed by in a blur. Rachel went to work every morning, spent time with her daughter, and slept most nights in Tyler's arms. He'd begun spending more time at Rachel's place in the evenings than his own. His SEAL team had two short missions, and each time he returned, they'd made love more passionately than before. Rachel was practically beaming with happiness every morning, dropping Keira off at school and then heading into work. Tyler left extremely early for PT, and she'd gotten used to him kissing her gently when he woke up, telling her to go back to sleep, and then quietly leaving her place to head in.

She'd gotten together with Addison once more while the men were gone, and she was meeting up with Addison and her friends for happy hour this evening. Tyler had offered to watch Keira for Rachel, and although she was a little surprised he'd be willing to do so, she'd accepted. Keira loved him, and she appreciated the chance to both let her daughter and boyfriend bond and get to know her new friends better.

Rachel pulled open the door to a popular seafood restaurant down by the water. The entire space was open and modern, and there was a sleek bar at the center. She spotted the petite brunette sitting at the bar with Olivia. The jet-black haired woman spotted her and waved. "Girl, get over here!" Olivia called out. "We just ordered a round of martinis."

Rachel crossed the busy restaurant, sliding onto a barstool and saying hello to the other women.

"You like martinis, right?" Addison asked. "Olivia already ordered us a round."

"Sounds perfect," Rachel assured her.

"Addison said you got your man to watch Keira tonight? He's a keeper." Olivia said with a grin.

Rachel smiled, accepting the drink the bartender slid toward her. "Keira loves Tyler. I wish she felt the same way about her dad, but that situation is still just weird."

"I'm sorry," Addison said, brushing her dark hair back. She wore dark eyeliner that made her brown eyes really pop. Rachel was blonde and blue-eyed, and she loved the mysterious look Addison seemed to give off. "She's still just going to visit him for the day, right?"

"Yep, but school is ending, so she's going to have overnights soon. The thing is, Kyle doesn't even seem too interested in Keira. He and Carly got engaged, and I swear that woman is always gushing about them

152

doing things together. Yet from what Keira says, she mostly plays alone."

"Maybe she wants kids and is trying to pretend she'll be a good mom," Addison mused. "She got him to propose, didn't she?"

"Maybe she's a gold-digger," Olivia said, taking a sip of her martini. "She's young, from what you've said. Maybe she's marrying your ex for his money. She's as fake as her false eyelashes and acrylic nails but is putting on a show to snag a husband."

"She is really vain," Rachel hedged. "She's into her designer purses and shoes, and Kyle bought her a ridiculously large engagement ring."

"And no doubt your ex is into her because she's young," Olivia said. "Some men really want a younger woman fawning over them. It's a huge ego boost. Is she blonde? You are," she pointed out, gesturing toward Rachel. "Maybe he has a 'type' of woman he goes for, and Carly checks all the boxes."

"I just hate that my daughter is caught in the middle of it." She frowned, looking around the crowded bar. Other people were talking and laughing, and this was supposed to be a fun evening. She didn't want to bring the others down.

"I don't mean to change the subject, but did I tell you I'm meeting Ace's parents this weekend?" Addison asked, grinning.

"What?" Olivia shrieked. "Girl, that man is crazy about you. Meeting the parents is a big step. Shoot, before we know it, you two will be getting hitched. All those guys on the other SEAL team are married or engaged, right? Ace will be next. I know it."

Addison flushed but smiled at them. "I don't know. It's too soon for marriage talk, but we'll see what happens. We're going to fly out to see my family, too. Ace already bought plane tickets for us. I can't wait for him to meet my mom. She'll absolutely love him. My dad will probably just think no one is good enough for his little girl, but eh. He's divorcing my mom, so clearly he's clueless about relationships."

"That sucks," Rachel said. "It's awesome you and Ace will meet each other's families though. That's a huge step."

"I'm excited. And Tyler seems crazy into you," she said with a smile. "I ran into him the other day, and he was going on and on about how awesome you and Keira are."

"Yes, girl, spill," Olivia said with a wicked grin as she leaned closer. "I can't rely on Owen for all my information."

"Owen?" Rachel asked, confused.

"Havoc," Addison explained. "Ace and I were going to dinner one night, and somehow Olivia and Owen—Havoc—ended up coming along. I'm not sure if I should get those two a referee or a hotel room," she added with a laugh.

"Oh, please. He only wishes he could have someone like me," Olivia said, flipping her dark hair back over her shoulder. "I don't date players. He's not serious about a thing and would never commit. I do have a feeling he'd be good in bed though. If I'm ever desperate, I'll take that for a ride."

"Oh my God," Rachel murmured as Addison nearly choked on her drink.

"I think he's actually a decent guy," Addison said. "More bark than bite, you know? He likes living up to his name and causing trouble."

"So where's Cassie?" Rachel asked. "Is she coming tonight? I haven't seen her for a few weeks."

"She's not coming," Olivia said. "And she was working from home today, so I didn't see her in the office either. We need to get her out of her apartment more."

"I'm worried about her," Addison admitted. "I'm sure Tyler told you the story about how I was kidnapped, right?"

"He did. I'm so sorry you ever went through that," Rachel said with a shudder. "You're amazingly strong."

"I'm not," Addison said. "Luckily Ace and the guys found me rather quickly. I was positively terrified. But apparently, Cassie was really freaking out that day. She'd been a little more subdued before that, but I don't know. I feel like she hasn't been the same."

Rachel frowned. "I wonder if she's okay. You two are close, right? Maybe your being kidnapped really upset her."

"Yeah, I think it did. But it's almost like it triggered something else. I don't know. I'm not a psychologist, and honestly, we were all growing closer then. I didn't know her too well before that."

"Next time, we'll make her come out with us," Olivia promised. "I'll go grab her from her apartment if I have to. Or maybe have Rob show up with me. I'm not sure what's going on between them, but he seems to know more than she's shared with us."

"Well, I don't know about you ladies, but I'm hungry. Should we order some food, too?" Addison asked.

"Absolutely. Tyler is feeding Keira dinner tonight, so I fully plan to enjoy my evening out. I love seafood, so I can't wait to check out the menu."

"Let's see if we can get a table," Olivia said, "unless you guys would rather eat at the bar?"

"Table," Addison agreed. "It's quieter there."

Olivia slid off her barstool, heading toward the hostess stand. A few pairs of male eyes slid her way. She seemed to know she had the attention of some of the men here and smiled as Rachel shook her head. Not many women had the confidence Olivia did. Rachel would never be the type of person who wanted all eyes on her, and she was totally fine with that.

"I'm glad things are going so well with you and Tyler. He's a good guy. Have you met the CO yet?" Addison asked.

"No, not yet," Rachel admitted.

"Well, his fiancée was involved in a crazy situation as well. Slate was having her stay at his place while some domestic terrorists were tracking him. The guys took turns staying with her at first, but she especially liked Tyler. Not that she was attracted to him," Addison hastily assured Rachel. "He's just easygoing and friendly. Everyone gets along with him."

"It's funny how we talked for nearly a year and didn't realize we were interested in each other. I mean, the man's gorgeous," Rachel said. "I always thought he was cute. But he's nice and funny, too. I assumed he'd have no interest in me since he's young and unattached. I feel like some men in their twenties wouldn't necessarily want to date a woman with a five-year-old."

"He's almost thirty," Addison said. "It's not like these guys are eighteen and fresh out of boot camp."

"Yeah, you're right," Rachel said with a laugh. "I guess when I was younger, I was just with the wrong men."

"Plus, timing is everything, too. Maybe you were busy with your daughter then and not ready for a relationship. She's in Kindergarten now, right? I don't know much about kids, but I could see that having a baby or young child would be even more work."

"Absolutely. And Tyler thought I was with Kyle, so, yeah. I'm glad we finally got on the same page."

"We'll have another barbeque soon," Addison said. "You guys had to leave quickly before. Maybe it'll just be Ace and Tyler's team. Last time we had everyone over, and it was a bit chaotic. Fun though."

Rachel took a sip of her martini and saw Olivia crossing toward them. "I got a table. Come on!" Rachel pulled some money from her wallet, setting it on the bar, and slid down from her barstool. She'd quick check her phone to make sure Tyler hadn't texted and then enjoy dinner with her friends. It felt good to have someone she trusted to watch her daughter. It was amazing how relaxed she felt—the complete opposite of when she sent Keira off with Kyle.

Her heart swelled as she thought of how well Tyler and Keira got along. Was it too much to hope that someday they'd be their own little family? It was still early in their relationship. She'd never really considered dating or marrying while Keira was young. It was just the two of them, and she was okay with it. Tyler had changed her entire world though. It was hard to imagine her life without him in it.

# Chapter 16

Tyler climbed into his pick-up truck the next day, grabbing his cell phone as it buzzed. "Hey, what's up man?" he asked as he saw Mark's name on the screen. He set the bag of groceries he'd been holding on the passenger seat, pulling his door shut.

"Not much," Mark said. "I just finished lifting. I prefer working out on base, but there are plenty of pretty girls hanging out around my apartment complex's gym."

Tyler burst into laughter. "Damn. I should've thought of that years ago. Our gym is so bad, I never bothered. Not that I need to meet a woman now."

"Hell no. Rachel is a knock-out. Sweet, too. I was surprised there were women here, but I happened to go by it the other night when I was dropping off some papers at the rental office. A few of them were working out, but one was standing around snapping selfies."

Tyler chuckled. "What was my sister doing there?"

"Ha. She was blonde. Could've been."

"Nah, she's not here yet. And there'd be no reason for her to show up at your apartment complex. Everly is supposed to come next weekend. She's staying in a nice hotel though, not slumming it at my place."

"Damn. Here I was knocking her being a blogger, but I guess she does all right."

"Yeah, don't worry. She can take care of herself. Ace and Addison are talking about having another barbeque soon, so maybe she'll meet everyone then. Or we could do the bonfire thing again. How'd you do at the meet market?" he joked. "Was your apartment gym filled with beautiful women today?"

"Mission failure. There were several women there the other night. Today, I decided to lift, and there was only another dude in the gym. I need to go in the evenings I guess."

"I can ask Rachel if she has any single friends. She's been hanging out with Addison and that group recently, but maybe she knows some lawyers."

"Nah. Too uptight."

"Suit yourself. Rach and I are having a day date today."

"A day date? What the hell is that?" Mark asked with a laugh.

"Keira is at her dad's house today. She hasn't been in a couple weeks because they were traveling. Rachel is kind of sad to send her there again, so I picked up some things at the store to cheer her up."

"Condoms?"

"Don't be an ass. I grabbed some wine, food she likes, and of course chocolate. All women love that. We're going to relax and enjoy the afternoon."

"I guess it wouldn't be cool to bribe the women at the gym with chocolate, right?" Mark joked. "I definitely won't be flashing condoms around."

"Hell no," Tyler agreed. "Not if you want a date. They'll think you're the crazy guy who lives there. Every place has one, right?"

Mark chuckled. "I'll catch you later then. Brian and I are heading to the beach. Havoc might come, too. If you've got alone time planned with your girl, I won't even bother inviting you along."

Tyler's lips quirked. Hell no, he wouldn't be hanging out with his buddies when he had a free afternoon with Rachel. Despite Mark's messing around with him, he actually had gotten condoms, too. He'd have a picnic lunch with Rachel, and then they'd enjoy some alone time for a couple of hours. They were always careful to be quiet, not wanting to wake Keira up, when he stayed overnight at her place. He'd love to see Rach completely let loose today. He loved kissing and pleasuring her, and making his woman cry out in passion. Tyler planned to make sure she was thoroughly sated this afternoon. He was generally an easygoing guy, but when he set his mind to something, he was all in. Making his woman lose her mind in bed definitely appealed to him.

He said goodbye to Mark and started his pick-up truck, glancing down to see a text from Rachel that had just popped up on his phone.

*Can't wait to see you, baby.*

He smiled, quickly thumbing a response.

*Me either. Be home soon.*

Home. He still lived next door, but it did feel like coming home. And he didn't mean his own sterile apartment. He loved her home—the cozy decorations, the kid stuff that still crept out of Keira's room, and mostly the smiles and laughter. He loved that he had Rachel and Keira in his life, and he had a feeling the best was yet to come.

***

Rachel slipped on her sandals, smoothing down her sundress. Tyler had wanted to have a picnic that afternoon, and she was looking forward to some special time together. Kyle had been down in Mexico a few weeks with Carly. She wasn't sure what exactly they'd been doing—an extended vacation? They'd recently gotten engaged, much to Rachel's dismay. A part of her had hoped their relationship would fizzle out. Then at least she wouldn't have to deal with Carly anymore. Their wedding planning was moving ahead though, whether she liked it or not. Both of them had been here when they'd picked up Keira, Carly once again gushing about how much she loved kids. Rachel had noticed the huge diamond solitaire on her finger. Of course. Kyle hadn't bothered to stick around when he'd gotten Rachel pregnant, but he'd proposed to this woman. Carly had gone on and on about the fun they'd have today. It was a little strange, given she'd been the one saying they'd eventually hire a nanny to watch her.

She brushed her long hair, catching the gleam of her tiny earrings in the light. Tyler seemed to love jewelry on her. She didn't think men usually noticed that sort of thing, but he'd been intrigued. She was almost tempted to pierce her belly button again. She'd had it done when she was in college but removed it when she was pregnant and then never bothered with it again. She sensed Tyler would've loved discovering that on her. She wasn't into tattoos, but it might be fun to get a temporary one just to surprise him someday. She'd let him discover it as he slowly undressed her.

Rachel swiped on some lip gloss, turning around in the mirror to see her sundress from all sides. It looked good, hugging her breasts just so and flaring out from hips. Tyler knocked on her door, and she hurried to the front of the apartment. He was grinning as she pulled open the door, holding a grocery bag and bottle of wine. Tyler hadn't shaved today, and her gaze raked over the stubble on his jaw. "I didn't shave," he said needlessly, watching her.

"It looks good. Sexy," she said, nervously biting her lip.

He chuckled, coming into her apartment. "Is that so? I thought we could eat first, but damn. You look good enough to eat, Rach." Her cheeks pinkened, and he set the wine and grocery bag of food down, pulling her toward him for a kiss. Her phone began buzzing, and she grabbed it from the table.

*We'll be late bringing Keira back.*

"Huh," she said, puzzling over his message. It wasn't that Kyle had never been late before, but it seemed odd he'd text her so early in the day announcing they'd be later than expected.

"What's wrong?" Tyler asked. She showed him the text, and he lifted a shoulder. "Did they go somewhere for the afternoon? Like to a movie or whatever?"

"I'm not sure. I was happy this was still just a day visit and didn't ask too many questions. We'll have to start the overnights soon. Poor Keira was crying about it. I've tried mentioning it a few times, just so she'd be prepared, but it seems to have backfired." She thumbed a text into her phone.

*What are you doing today?*

Kyle didn't answer, and her gaze flicked to Tyler. "He's not responding. I never really worried about it before, it's just…. I don't know."

"You want me to have Ace track them down? I bet he could find them if Kyle doesn't respond. He could track their cells or even get into the car's GPS. No doubt Kyle's BMW has navigation built in."

"What? No," she said quickly. "They haven't even been gone for long. I always worry when he picks her up. I'm just extra nervous since this is the last regular visit, you know? Next time I'll have to pack her an overnight bag and deal with not seeing her until the next day. I'm just stressed."

"Hey," he said in a low voice, running his fingers up her bare arm. "You're an amazing mom. You're worried because you care about her. It'll be hard at first when she spends nights away from you, but hell. I'll be here to hold you close."

"Yeah?" she asked, swiping a tear away as she looked up at him.

"Absolutely. Actually, you might need some up close and personal attention right now," he said huskily, moving closer. Tyler's arms wrapped around her, and then he was ducking lower, kissing her gently. One hand gripped her hip, the other sliding to palm the back of her head. He kissed her again, more deeply, and she felt her nipples tighten.

"How about I stick this food in your fridge?" he asked. "I'll bring some glasses of wine back to your bedroom, and we can relax in there instead. After I make love to you, we'll have an indoor picnic."

"A picnic on my bed?" she asked with a giggle.

"Um-hmm. Except we'll both be wearing a lot less clothes."

"All right. You've convinced me, sailor man. Go pop the cork on the bottle of wine, and I'll meet you in my bedroom in a few minutes."

# Chapter 17

Tyler smiled, running his hand over Rachel's blonde tresses. She was sprawled out on top of him in bed, lightly sleeping. She'd had another brief round of tears earlier, but he'd kissed her thoroughly, making her forget about everything but his touches and kisses for the moment.

They'd made love twice, once with Tyler holding her against the bedroom wall while he eagerly bucked into her. She'd clung to him, those slender legs wrapped around his waist, crying out his name. The second time had been slower. Sweeter. He'd spread her beneath him in bed, capturing her cries with his mouth and slowly moving in and out of her welcoming body until Rachel had begged him for more. His cock had been rock-hard, but he'd kept his slow pace, strumming her clit and feeling her pussy clench down around him as he eased in and out.

When neither of them had been able to take it anymore, Tyler had finally thrust faster. He'd pressed his fingers against her clit, thrusting in deep, and she'd exploded, bucking wildly beneath him. Tyler's orgasm had immediately followed, and he'd rolled them over, holding her close.

He gently played with her hair some more, watching as the sunlight slanted through the blinds. It was getter later. They'd enjoyed a picnic of cheese, appetizers, and chocolate, plus a bottle of her favorite wine. Tyler was more of a beer guy, but it had been romantic sipping wine naked together in bed. Rachel's long, blonde hair had curled around her breasts. She had light-colored nipples, and she was so sensitive, he swore someday he could probably make her come just from touching and kissing her gorgeous breasts.

His phone buzzed with a message, and as he glanced at the quick text from Ace, he realized it was already nineteen hundred. Keira was originally due back at eighteen hundred, but Kyle had said they'd be late. It was already an hour later than originally planned though.

Should he wake Rachel? Go check her phone for any messages?

Gently easing her body off of his, he tugged the covers back around her and stood. She looked so gorgeous, her hair spread out across the pillow, her breasts pillowed against the sheets. His cock was still semi-hard as he crossed her bedroom. At the last moment, he turned and grabbed his boxers from the floor. Rachel's phone was still in the living room, and he didn't want Kyle showing up while he was out there buck naked.

He strode down the hallway of her apartment, spotting her phone on the table right by the front door. Picking it up, he swiped the screen. He knew she kept it unlocked so Keira could play on it sometimes. Tyler wasn't one to snoop through someone else's things, but he wanted to quick check and make sure Kyle hadn't tried calling or texting.

Frowning, he saw she had some texts from a group chat with her friends, but that was it. There were no missed calls either. He didn't read any of her private messages, just carried the phone back to the bedroom. Rachel gently stirred, and he sank onto the bed beside her. She shifted slightly, the sheet moving lower across her breasts. Tyler's cock twitched, but he ignored it. "Hey, baby. It's already seven. I just grabbed your phone but don't see any messages from Kyle."

"What?" she asked, groggily sitting up in bed. The sheet fell, baring her breasts, and she clutched at it. Tyler reached down, swiping his own tee shirt off the floor, and handing it to her. Although he loved gazing at her body, he wanted her to feel comfortable. She quickly tugged on his tee shirt, the soft material clinging to her breasts. It was too big on her, but damn if he didn't love seeing Rachel in his clothing. "Kyle didn't call?"

"I don't think so," he said in a low voice. "We both fell asleep. When I realized how late it was, I went to grab your phone and see if he'd texted."

"Okay," she said, taking it from him. Rachel frowned as she swiped the screen. "I'll send him a text. They're probably just running later than expected." She quickly thumbed a message and sent it as Tyler sat there on her bed. For the first time, he felt guilty for distracting her all afternoon. What if something was wrong? They'd had a couple glasses of wine, made love, and drowsily fallen asleep in each other's arms.

Should they have questioned Kyle when he said they'd be late? He'd never responded to Rachel's text. Maybe Tyler should've contacted Ace then. His buddy could've easily located them, putting Rachel's and his minds at ease.

Tyler stood, grabbing his own phone from the nightstand. He texted Ace, asking if he'd be able to run a trace on Kyle's cell. It was likely unnecessary. They were probably on their way back right now. That didn't stop his gut from churning though. He hated the worry on Rachel's face. And for a man that was used to being alert, he felt like he'd let his guard down. They knew Keira would be gone for the day, so they'd enjoyed some time alone as a couple.

"Do you have Carly's number?" he asked.

"No," she said, frowning. She bit her lip, her eyebrows creasing. "I'll just try calling Kyle. He didn't answer my text, but they're probably on their way back." She pushed the call button, freezing as it went straight to voicemail. "His phone's turned off."

Tyler stared at her, worry coursing through him. He was already running multiple scenarios through his mind. "Maybe his battery died. Ace can still probably ping his cell. Even if it's not turned on now, we'll know his last location."

Rachel swallowed, and he hated the worry on her face. "Okay. Let's do that."

Tyler texted Ace again. His team leader promised to quick look into it. Addison was into coding, so she'd probably be able to help if she was with him. Both of them were scary smart when it came to computers. His phone buzzed with an incoming call, and he lifted it to his ear, staring down at Rachel, who was still sitting on the bed in his tee shirt. "Hey, man. Any luck?"

"Yeah, and it's not good. The last location his cell phone pinged was at LAX."

"The airport?" Tyler asked, bewildered.

"Affirmative. He was there at oh-eleven-hundred. The phone's been turned off since."

"Shit," Tyler muttered, pacing the bedroom. Rachel jumped up and hurried toward him. "What's wrong? What happened?"

Tyler put the phone on speaker. "Rach is here with me," he explained. She clutched onto his arm, standing close at his side. Her blonde hair was rumpled from their afternoon spent in bed, but he couldn't even appreciate the tempting sight of her in his tee shirt anymore—not when Keira might be in danger.

"I tracked Kyle's cell phone," Ace explained to her. "It's turned off, as you already know, but it pings the nearby cell towers when it is on. The last location was at LAX earlier this morning. His phone has been off since then."

"Holy shit!" Rachel said, stepping back in surprise. "He took her to the airport? Oh my God." She paled, and Tyler reached out to grip her arm, steadying her.

"Easy, baby," he murmured. "Sit back down, and we'll figure this out."

"I have to call my lawyer," she said in a daze. "He's not allowed to take her anywhere outside of San Diego. Or the police. The airport police. TSA?"

Tyler took the phone off speaker, lifting it to his ear, and guided Rachel back to her bed. He sank down beside her, his hand landing on her bare thigh. "Breathe, Rach. We don't know what's going on.

Maybe he dropped Carly off at the airport," Tyler said, doubting that was true. He spoke quietly into the phone with Ace, who planned to contact the rest of their teammates. Rachel was already texting someone on her own phone, presumably her lawyer.

"Listen," he said, as soon as he'd gotten off the call. "Rob is up that way anyway today. He took off for a drive up the coast. He's going to head to LAX. We've got some contacts there, so he'll touch base with them in person and find out what's going on. Addison will get Carly's number, and they'll run a trace on that phone as well. Mark is going to Kyle's house. Maybe this was all some big misunderstanding."

"It's not," she said. "You know it's not. They took her to the airport."

Tyler took her hand, squeezing it gently. "We have to check everything, Rach. All possibilities. Ace is already hacking into the DMV database to get Kyle's license plates. Ace can track his vehicle from the highway cameras. It's all automated, so that can be running in the background while we're looking. We'll see if they came back this way at some point. We'll also be contacting the airlines. We still don't know what's going on, Rach. Maybe they're late because they drove up to L.A."

"He's not supposed to leave the San Diego area," she whispered, tears smarting her eyes. "He knew what he was doing. They both came to get her today, and Kyle texted to say he'd be late. They planned this." A few tears slipped down her cheeks, and Tyler had never felt more helpless. He pulled her against him, his hand running down her back as she trembled.

"Did you contact your lawyer?" he asked in a low voice.

"Yes. She said to call the police if they're not here soon. It could be considered a kidnapping for violating the court's visitation schedule. She's going to contact his lawyer, too, but oh my God," she murmured, burying her head into Tyler's bare shoulder as her tears fell. "They took my baby." He held Rachel, trying to soothe her, but he hated feeling so helpless. Tyler didn't know what was going on either. He wanted to rush out the door, straight to Keira, but at this point, no one knew where she was. They needed a definite lead to move in. Had they flown somewhere in the U.S.? Taken her out of the country?

Had Tyler been spending a lazy afternoon in bed with Rachel while her daughter was being taken somewhere against her will? She might've been five, but she was still a young child. Kidnappings of young children were often committed by people they knew—by family members. Had her own damn father kidnapped her?

A loud knocking on her door had them both jumping in surprise. Tyler tugged on his shorts, moving toward the front of the apartment. He was shirtless, but he didn't give a fuck. Blinking in surprise, Tyler stared at Havoc as he yanked open the door.

"Ace just called me. What do you guys need?"

Tyler frowned, at a loss for maybe the first time ever. He was used to making a plan and figuring things out. To gathering all the intelligence needed to move in without having any doubts. At the moment, he felt so damn helpless it hurt. "I guess we should check Kyle's house," he finally murmured. "Mark headed over, but you guys might need to break in. Maybe we can find something there."

"On it. How's Rachel?"

"Upset. Scared. It's not that late yet, but hell. Kyle texted her earlier today saying they'd be later than planned. That should've sent up all sorts of red flags, but we just went with it."

"It's not your fault," Havoc assured him. "Text me his address, and I'll check it out. Rob will be at LAX in under thirty minutes. He can talk to the authorities there."

"Roger," Tyler said as Havoc turned and left, feeling slightly off-kilter. Tyler was used to training with his teammates, being put in dangerous, physical situations, but this situation was throwing him for a loop. His gut told him it wasn't an innocent misunderstanding of arriving back later than expected. Kyle had fucking taken Rachel's daughter. Kidnapped her. Tyler would never forgive himself if something happened to that little girl. He loved both Rachel and Keira more than he ever thought possible, and Tyler knew he'd do whatever was necessary to get her back.

# Chapter 18

"How are you doing?" Addison asked, handing Rachel a steaming cup of tea. It was three in the morning, and the women had all camped out at Rachel's apartment. She'd pulled on her joggers and a sweatshirt, not able to warm up. The chill seeping through her was bone deep.

It had been hours since Kyle was supposed to return with Keira. Hours and hours. When they'd finally gotten the authorities involved, they'd learned Kyle and Carly had boarded a flight with Keira down to Mexico. Rather than crossing the land border just south of San Diego, they'd caught a flight from L.A. to Cancun, then simply vanished.

"Why the hell would he take her?" Rachel asked, tears slipping down her cheeks. She set the mug of tea down on the coffee table. "He didn't even want her. It's a horrible thing to say, but it's true. He wasn't here when she was born. He didn't see any baby pictures or want to cuddle with her or feed her a bottle. He literally just dumped us like we were nothing. I won't pretend Kyle and I were serious about each other, but my God. She was his child, and he deserted her."

"They'll get her back," Addison said. "Ace said they were already working with the FBI and Mexican authorities to track them down."

"It's taking too long," Rachel whispered, swiping away her tears. "Tyler told me that story of when their CO's fiancée was kidnapped. The guys drove down to Tijuana and found her rather quickly in a house there. Keira's been gone since this morning, and she's just a little girl."

"Cancun's farther than Tijuana though," Olivia pointed out. "A lot of that time was in the air. They got a jump on us, for sure, but the guys know what they're doing."

"You know Tyler will do everything he can to find her," Addison said. "He's not going to rest until he brings her back. That man is absolutely crazy in love with you."

Rachel looked over at her, sniffling. "We haven't even told each other that yet. I mean, he's over here every single night. I should have told him how I feel."

"He knows," Addison assured her.

"What's Carly have on Kyle anyway?" Olivia mused.

"What do you mean?" Addison asked. She took a sip of her own tea, watching Olivia.

"Why would he go to all this trouble for her, you know? She's young and probably likes to suck his dick or whatever, but damn."

"Olivia!" Cassie chastised, frowning. Rachel had

been shocked when she'd shown up with the others, but whatever funk she'd been in, she'd snapped out of to offer her support. Although Rachel didn't know her as well as Addison and Olivia, she appreciated her being here.

"I just mean, he's buying her expensive things, bending over backwards to make her happy. If she's the one who pushed him into seeing Keira after all these years, what was it about? Why's he willing to do whatever Carly wants?"

Rachel blew out a sigh. "I don't know. None of it makes sense. I think she just wanted to get married and lock him down, you know? She likes his money. If she dangles Keira in front of him, she's giving him a family—sort of. Or getting an instant family. She's totally fake, but maybe she wants to look like she's a good wife and mom. Oh God. If they get married, she would be Keira's stepmom."

"Not anymore," Olivia said. "They'll both be in jail."

There was a knock on the apartment door, and then Rob strode in, glancing around at the women. "I told Ace I'd come over here," he said, his gaze briefly moving from Rachel to Cassie. "I spent a few hours at LAX then drove straight here. Where's Trigger?"

"At Kyle's house with the police," Rachel said. "I'm sure you saw one officer outside the door. The others just left. They got a search warrant. I think Mark and Havoc wanted to get in earlier but were waiting for the police. Tyler rushed straight there. I told him I was fine waiting here with the girls. I think he really needed to go and do something. Waiting around isn't his style."

"That sounds about right," Rob said, his voice

low. "Mind if I sit for a minute?"

"Of course," Rachel said, gesturing toward an empty chair.

Rob crossed over toward it, and she saw Cassie watching him closely. "I saw the security footage from the airport. For what it's worth, Keira wasn't upset right then. I know that doesn't mean much, but I thought it might make you feel better," he said, those intense eyes landing on her.

She let out a shaky breath. "Yeah, a little. I'm sure she's scared now though. Hopefully she fell asleep. It's the middle of the night. I feel awful knowing every second she might be hurting. Not that I think they'd physically harm her, but I'm sure she's got to be terrified. And after what they pulled off today? You just never know."

"Ace looked further into Carly's background," Rob said. "I just got off the phone with him when I was checking in. Apparently, she's deep in debt. She'd stolen someone's identity to open up multiple credit lines. She's maxed those cards out and still wanted more. None of it showed up in the background check since it was using a different name."

"Jesus," Olivia murmured. "What a bitch."

"Kyle emptied his bank accounts," Rob said. "It sounds like they were planning this for a while."

"What does this have to do with Keira though?" Cassie asked. "They just wanted a kid?"

Rachel shrugged helplessly. "I wish I knew."

"Maybe she can't have kids," Addison said.

Rob's gaze slid to her. "So, she'd kidnap another woman's child?"

"I don't know," Addison said. "Maybe she couldn't get pregnant or didn't want to. She's drowning in debt but wants a family and fake life. I'm not saying it's logical, but the woman sounds nuts."

Olivia looked over at Rob. "You said she's in debt. Did Kyle know that?"

"It's a good question, but I just don't know. He could've emptied his bank accounts because they planned to flee the country with Keira."

"It seems like he'd do anything for Carly. That makes me think she's got dirt on him or something," Olivia said.

Rachel puzzled over Olivia's comment. Kyle did seem intent on making her happy and buying her expensive things, but goodness. Carly was young with big boobs and a perfect body. Maybe he just wanted to get laid. Not that he couldn't find other willing women, but some men wouldn't mind having a young blonde waiting in their bed every night. No doubt Carly probably gushed over Kyle, making him feel important.

Rob's phone buzzed, and he lifted it to his ear. "Yeah. Yeah. What? Fucking hell. Okay. I'll be right over." He stood, looking at the women. "Trigger just called. They found some interesting intel at Kyle's. Apparently, he's fathered multiple other children over the years but denied responsibility and skipped out on child support in most cases. Somehow, Carly found all this out and seems to have confronted him about it."

"What?" Rachel asked, her jaw dropping.

Rob's lips pressed together in a thin line as he nodded. "Yep. I don't know if his paternity has been proven in every instance, but Trigger said she had files spread across the kitchen table. I'm guessing she blackmailed Kyle. That's why he was willing to do whatever she wanted. Carly's using him for his money, and she's got him right where she wants him. He's a musician, right? Kyle's popular with the locals, even though he never hit it bigtime. He's worried it would ruin his career if this got leaked to the press. I don't know how many children he's fathered, but he could owe huge amounts of back child support."

"Plus whatever credit card bills Carly's been running up," Olivia commented.

"What a prick," Rachel said. "I can't believe this. He's an even bigger jackass than I thought."

Rob eyed her. "Yep. Trigger doesn't like how long the FBI is taking. Sometimes in situations like this, men can get desperate. If Kyle realizes the authorities are moving in—"

"Oh my God—Keira!" Rachel cried out.

"Shhh," Addison said, wrapping an arm around her shoulder. "They'll find her."

"Ace got the location of a house. Don't ask me how—that guy's a genius. Trigger and I are flying down to Mexico ourselves," Rob said. "We'll get her back."

Rachel's cell phone began buzzing, and she hastily grabbed it, listening to Tyler confirm what Rob had just told her. Somehow, Ace had gotten their suspected location. She didn't even understand half of what Tyler was telling her. All that mattered was that he was about to go rescue her daughter. Her Navy SEAL boyfriend and his teammate were about to go on an unsanctioned mission to get Keira back. She hated that they were potentially risking their careers over this, but she knew Tyler wouldn't stand down.

"I love Keira like I love you, baby," Tyler said, his voice thick with emotion. "I know I haven't said it yet, but I'd do anything for you. I'm heading straight to the airport. The next time you see me, I'll have our girl."

"Okay," she said, tears streaming down her cheeks. "Please be careful."

"I will. I love you, Rachel."

"I love you, too. But are you sure about this? It's so dangerous, and you could get in major trouble. I don't want you going to jail or something."

"I'm sure. I'd never let anything happen to either of you. Rob and I will get her back, I swear. You stay put, okay? The girls will stay with you. Ace is looking into various systems from base. Havoc's staying here at Kyle's, but Mark is headed to you to wait there until I get back."

"Okay," she said, letting out a deep breath.

Tyler seemed to realize how stressed she was. "Just breathe, baby. This will all be over soon. I'll bring Keira home to you."

"She means everything to me, Tyler. Everything."

"I know, because you both mean everything to me. I love you, Rach, and I'll be home with her soon."

He ended the call, and she tearfully looked around at her friends. Rob had already hurried out the door to meet up with Tyler. Addison squeezed Rachel's hand as the other women huddled close. "They'll find her," Addison whispered. "Our guys will get her back."

# Chapter 19

The balmy Mexican breeze blew against Tyler's face as he and Rob crouched down in position. They'd flown in to Cancun early that morning, not waiting for the U.S. and Mexican authorities to work out a compromise on extraditing Keira. The fact that Kyle was her father posed a problem, but he was an American citizen, not Mexican. It would've been more difficult otherwise. Tyler wasn't waiting around for the State Department and FBI to figure out a plan. They were still dicking around, trying to determine where Keira had been taken. Ace had hacked further into Kyle's phone records, tracking his movements over the past few weeks. The GPS location in Mexico had given them everything they'd needed. It turned out that Kyle's previous trip here with Carly had provided them exactly what they needed. If he hadn't traveled here recently, they might not have found Keira so fast.

Tyler glanced over at his teammate. Rob had been pissed as hell that Rachel's ex had kidnapped Keira. He'd come straight from Rachel's place to the airport, meeting Tyler there for a pre-dawn flight. They'd left U.S. military bases in the middle of the night plenty of times over their careers. This was different though. More significant. Tyler was used to being in control, with all of his teammates surrounding him. He hated the nerves he felt now.

"You okay?" Rob asked, his green gaze penetrating.

Tyler nodded. "Yep. I'm ready to do this. That little girl didn't deserve any of this—not her jackass of a father disappearing, not him suddenly pretending to care after five years, and certainly not being kidnapped and taken from her mother."

"It should be a fairly simple grab," Rob said. "Neither of them have any sort of training. We don't know if they're armed though. Desperate people can do desperate things."

"Don't I know it," Tyler muttered. "My only priority is Keira. Those other two can rot in jail or a shallow grave for all that I care."

Tyler felt on edge moving in without the rest of his teammates or all of his gear. He and Rob had needed to appear as normal as they could. Although they had small earpieces in, and sidearms, they weren't in full body armor. Both men were wearing Kevlar vests under their clothing, and they had combat boots on and their K-Bar knives. It should be an easy extraction—except they were dealing with a young, scared child.

Ace's voice came over their earpieces. "We don't have drone imagery, obviously, but sat images from several hours ago show no one has come or gone. It should just be the three of them inside. The place was empty before Kyle showed up."

Tyler spoke into his mic in a low voice, watching the place in the early morning light.

Rob glanced at the large mansion. "Did Kyle buy this place?"

"Sounds like it, although he's got to be nearly broke by now. He must owe hundreds of thousands in back child support, plus he's got her shopping addiction to keep up with. She'd maxed out her credit cards, and from what Rachel said, he was lavishing Carly with gifts."

Rob shook his head. "It makes no sense. He and Carly could've just snuck off themselves without kidnapping a child."

Tyler's gaze landed on the mansion. "Yeah, I agree. I'm guessing she did really want a child, despite her crazed behavior, and Kyle was willing to do anything for her. No other explanation makes sense."

Ace spoke into their earpieces again, and Tyler nodded at Rob. It should be an easy in, with no special safeguards protecting the mansion. They'd breached all sorts of highly fortified buildings around the world over the years. This was just a man who'd fled the country out of desperation, taking his young child with him. Kyle was a musician, not a hardened criminal or terrorist. He didn't even own a gun, at least not legally, according to records. The man spent his time on his music, wooing his newest girlfriend and spending ridiculous amounts of money. He wasn't exactly some criminal mastermind.

"Affirmative," Tyler said into his mic as Ace finished his update.

"Let's roll," Rob said in confirmation.

They'd already made plans for Tyler to breach the front door while Rob headed around back. The FBI was still working with Mexican authorities, but they'd be in and out, rescuing Keira and then catching a flight with some counterparts at the DEA. They'd owe the guys they knew a few favors, but hell. It would be more than worth it to get Keira out of Mexico ASAP.

Tyler moved forward, his weapon in hand, approaching the silent mansion. He and Rob were about to give Kyle the shock of his lifetime. He just didn't want to scare Keira in the process. And Carly? Well, she could go eat a bag of dicks for all he cared. She was a leech, sucking out all that was good from the people around her. She'd been preoccupied with Keira for months, spending Kyle's money and trying to make them a family. Rachel's intuition had been right all along.

Rob spoke into his mic, indicating he was in position. Tyler gave the count, and then he was kicking in the door. No one came at him as he rushed inside, and he saw Rob moving in from the back of the house. They both glanced toward the stairs, and then they were taking them two at a time. Rob kicked open a door, and Tyler heard a woman's shriek pierce the early morning hours. Rob moved into Kyle and Carly's bedroom, but Tyler was already rushing down the hall, checking every room. At last he came to a door at the end, and he eased it open, weapon in hand.

His heart caught as he spotted Keira sleeping in her bed. Her blonde hair fanned out over the pillow, and she was clutching the blanket tightly in her arms. Tyler approached slowly, not wanting to scare her. That little girl was the most precious thing in the world to him. She and Rachel were everything, and he was about to bring her home.

Tyler spoke quietly into his mic and holstered his weapon, knowing Rob had the others under control.

"Keira," he said quietly, not wanting to shock her. "Hey, kiddo, it's me. Tyler. Wake up." He reached over and turned on the lamp, surprised she was still asleep. Then again, it had been a long and stressful day. The poor kid was no doubt exhausted. He just hoped she hadn't been too terrified by the ordeal. "Keira," he said again, a little louder. "Time to wake up, kiddo."

She finally stirred in her sleep, blinking as she began to take in her surroundings. She looked confused for a moment then flung herself at Tyler. "Mr. Tyler! You found me! I knew you would come and find me."

He caught her in his arms, tears smarting his eyes. "I did find you, sweetie," he said, standing up with her. She clung to him like a little koala bear, not willing to let go. He wouldn't have it any other way. With her tangled blonde hair and rumpled pajamas, she looked every bit the innocent child she was. Tyler couldn't believe her asshole of a father had kidnapped her. The only good news was, she'd never have to stay with Kyle and Carly again.

"Is Mommy here?" she asked, sleepily nuzzling against him.

"No, but we're going to go see her. We'll fly back home to California. Does that sound good?"

"I missed Mommy," she said, sniffling. "You too. Mr. Kyle said we were taking a fun trip, but then when we got on the airplane, Carly said I couldn't see Mommy again. I cried, and she told me to be a big girl."

"You are a big girl," Tyler assured her as he moved through the house. "You're the bravest kid I know." Rob was speaking to him over the headset, and Ace had promised to alert the local authorities.

Tyler kept moving through the immaculate mansion, not giving a shit about the money Kyle had or the fact that Rob had them both tied up in the bedroom. He could never afford something like this on his military salary, but it didn't matter. He had both Rachel and Keira's love, which was something that could never be bought. He'd do anything to protect them both, including traveling to the ends of the Earth to make sure they were safe.

"Tyler?" Keira asked, ducking her head against his shoulder as they moved into the early morning light.

"Yeah, sweetie?" he asked, heading straight toward their vehicle. Rob was already coming out the door after him, and they'd leave Kyle and Carly for the Mexican authorities to deal with.

"Will you be my daddy someday? I don't like Mr. Kyle. I'd rather you marry my mommy."

He ran his hand over her little blonde head, his heart clenching. This kid. There wasn't anything he wouldn't do for her. "I'd like that, Keira. I'll talk to your mom. There's nothing I want more than for the three of us to be a family."

# Epilogue

Keira shrieked with laughter as she raced around on the sand, the waves crashing on the shore in the distance. Tyler took Rachel's hand in his own, pulling her close. "I'd say this bonfire worked out okay."

She smiled up at him. "That'd be the understatement of the year. Keira's got your friends practically eating out of her hand. I certainly didn't expect Havoc of all people to have a soft spot for kids."

Tyler lifted a shoulder. "He's a kid at heart I guess, despite all the trouble he causes."

The salty breeze blew through her hair, and Tyler brushed a stray piece back, gazing into her eyes. "This has been a crazy few days. Did I tell you what Keira said when we were down in Mexico?"

Rachel stilled, searching his gaze. "No. What?"

"She said she wanted me to be her dad," Tyler said, lifting one hand and trailing his fingers over

Rachel's cheek. "I know it's a little soon for us to get engaged, but I'd love that, Rach. I'd love to call you my own and to adopt Keira someday."

"Oh Tyler," she said, tears smarting her eyes. "I still can't believe any of this."

"I hope those are happy tears," he said, ducking down for a soft kiss as his fingers slid into her hair.

"Of course they are," she assured him. "You risked your life and career to rescue my daughter. I love you more than anything—well, as much as Keira," she amended with a small laugh. "But I love you in different ways."

"I love you both, too," he said, his blue eyes gentle. "I'd kill anyone that hurt either of you. Maybe that sounds harsh or totally alpha, but I wouldn't have left Mexico without Keira."

"I know you wouldn't have. I don't know what I did to deserve you or how I could ever thank you enough for saving her. I love you so much."

He smiled, pulling Rachel close. His lips were at her ear, his voice husky as he spoke in a low voice. "I don't know, Rach. This morning was a pretty awesome thank you." Her cheeks heated as she recalled surprising Tyler in bed. He'd been asleep, and she'd tugged his boxer down, eagerly taking him into her mouth as he hardened. He'd nearly come after a minute of her attention, but he'd turned her over in bed and taken her from behind, one hand on her headboard for support, the other on her clit as he bucked into her.

Tyler loved to take control, and Rachel had to admit she loved that about him. He was big and broad and seemed to know exactly how to touch her body until she was practically desperate, begging him for relief. He loved making her come over and over, and she couldn't believe how attentive he still was in bed and how many different ways he loved to make love to her.

"What's up, lovebirds?" Mark joked, crossing over to them with a beer in hand. "I can't believe Keira has Havoc wrapped around her finger."

Rachel watched her daughter chasing the SEAL around the beach. He pretended she caught him, collapsing onto the sand with a series of dramatic groans. "I'm not sure which one of them is having more fun," she admitted.

"Havoc," both Tyler and Mark immediately replied as she burst into laughter.

Tyler's gaze landed on Mark, his lips quirking. "I know I was joking with you about staying away from my sister a few weeks ago, but hell. After the way you stayed with Rach the other night, making sure she was okay, I'll set you two up myself. Everly could use someone to ground her."

"Wait, you want to meet Everly?" Rachel asked, looking over at Mark in surprise.

"He saw her pictures on social media," Tyler said. "At first, I was annoyed he and Blaze had seen them, but hell. It's all public. Everly no doubt loves the attention. Of course, if I tell her she's got a Navy SEAL interested, no doubt it will go straight to her head."

Mark chuckled, taking a pull of his beer. "Nah. I mean, I appreciate that you'd trust me with your sister, man, but like I said. I couldn't deal with that sort of drama."

"Mommy, watch this!" Keira yelled from the beach, interrupting their conversation. She pretended to tackle Havoc and then Brian, who were having way more fun than they should've.

"Goodness," Rachel laughed. "Those two need girlfriends. They'll have the women chasing after them when they see how they act with kids."

"I told you you'd fit right in," Tyler said with a smile.

"You did, didn't you?" she asked, looking up into his eyes. Mark had already drifted away, talking with Olivia, Addison, and Ace near the bonfire. She had all that she wanted right in front of her though.

"Yep. Next week Everly will be here, and I'll probably be holding back the guys hitting on her. You fit into my life way more than my own sister ever will. She's completely different from me. You and Keira will always be my priority, no matter what. I hope you know I'd do anything for you."

"You already have. You've done everything and more. I love you, Tyler."

He ducked down for a soft kiss, and she felt the heat building between them, the incredible chemistry that was always there. She never totally grasped what it meant to have someone be both your friend and lover, but Tyler was it. He was her boyfriend, her best friend, and the man who made her knees weak from his kisses and caresses. Every time they made love, it was like their souls connected.

"I love you, too, Rach," he said, pressing even closer as his muscular arms tightened around her. "I love you more than you'll ever know."

# About the Author

USA Today Bestselling Author Makenna Jameison writes sizzling romantic suspense, including the addictive Alpha SEALs series.

Makenna loves the beach, strong coffee, red wine, and traveling. She lives in Washington DC with her husband and two daughters.

Visit www.makennajameison.com to discover your next great read.

Made in the USA
Coppell, TX
22 February 2022

73942516R00111